Praise for Cathie Linz

"Ms. Linz has the rare gift
of touching the ordinary with a quiet magic that
always makes our day shine a little brighter."
—*Romantic Times*

A familiar fire smoldered within him.

It wasn't the kind of flame that flared to life
the instant he saw her, but it was the kind that
grew in intensity each time he and Juliet were
together. Instant lust Luc could deal with, but
this overwhelmingly powerful attraction was
something else entirely.

"I should have worn black leather," he heard
her mutter and almost groaned aloud at the sexy
fantasy of her dressed like a biker babe—her
thighs barely covered by a short skirt, her breasts
pushing against a tight T-shirt. His body responded
to the hot images, forcing him to shift position on
the motorcycle, which only made her thighs rub
against his even more.

When had his sweet innocent Juliet turned into
such a sultry sex kitten?

Dear Reader,

Summer's finally here! Whether you'll be lounging poolside, at the beach, or simply in your home this season, we have great reads packed with everything you enjoy from Silhouette Romance—tenderness, emotion, fun and, of course, heart-pounding romance—plus some very special surprises.

First, don't miss the exciting conclusion to the thrilling ROYALLY WED: THE MISSING HEIR miniseries with Cathie Linz's *A Prince at Last!* Then be swept off your feet—just like the heroine herself!—in Hayley Gardner's *Kidnapping His Bride.*

Romance favorite Raye Morgan is back with *A Little Moonlighting,* about a tycoon set way off track by his beguiling associate who wants a family to call her own. And in Debrah Morris's *That Maddening Man,* can a traffic-stopping smile convince a career woman—and single mom—to slow down...?

Then laugh, cry and fall in love all over again with two incredibly tender love stories. Vivienne Wallington's *Kindergarten Cupids* is a very different, highly emotional story about scandal, survival and second chances. Then dive right into Jackie Braun's *True Love, Inc.,* about a professional matchmaker who's challenged to find her very sexy, very cynical client his perfect woman. Can she convince him that she already has?

Here's to a wonderful, relaxing summer filled with happiness and romance. See you next month with more fun-in-the-sun selections.

Happy reading!

Mary-Theresa Hussey

Mary-Theresa Hussey
Senior Editor

Please address questions and book requests to:
Silhouette Reader Service
U.S.: 3010 Walden Ave., P.O. Box 1325, Buffalo, NY 14269
Canadian: P.O. Box 609, Fort Erie, Ont. L2A 5X3

A Prince at Last!

CATHIE LINZ

SILHOUETTE *Romance*®

Published by Silhouette Books

America's Publisher of Contemporary Romance

Special thanks and acknowledgment are given to Cathie Linz for her
contribution to the ROYALLY WED: THE MISSING HEIR series.

For my senior editor, Mary-Theresa Hussey, for inviting me to
participate in this fun project, and for my editor, Allison Lyons, for
wining and dining me in New Orleans but especially for being so easy
to work with! Many thanks to you both!

 SILHOUETTE BOOKS

ISBN 0-373-19594-X

A PRINCE AT LAST!

Visit Silhouette at www.eHarlequin.com

Printed in U.S.A.

Books by Cathie Linz

CATHIE LINZ

left her career in a university law library to become a *USA Today* bestselling author of contemporary romances. She is the recipient of the highly coveted Storyteller of the Year Award given by *Romantic Times* and was recently nominated for a Love and Laughter Career Achievement Award for the delightful humor in her books.

Cathie often uses comic mishaps from her own trips as inspiration for her stories. After traveling, Cathie is always glad to get back home to her family, her two cats, her trusty word processor and her hidden cache of Oreo cookies!

THE DE BERGERONS OF ST. MICHEL

King Antoine de Bergeron (d)
m.
Queen Simone

1st marriage
Katie Graham (d)

LUC DUMONT m. JULIET BEAUDREAU
A Prince at Last!, SR #1594, 6/02

2nd marriage
Johanna Van Rhys (D)

Lise m. Charles Rodin
A Princess in Waiting, SR #1588, 5/02

Ariane m. Prince Etienne
In Pursuit of a Princess, SR #1582, 4/02

Marie-Claire m. Sebastian LeMarc
Of Royal Blood, SR #1576, 3/02

Georges
Juliet

3rd marriage
Helene Beaudreau (d)

Jacqueline

King Philippe

4th marriage
Celeste Buscari

Unborn Child

Key:
d Deceased
D Divorced
= Child from previous marriage

Chapter One

"I'm having a bad heir day," Luc Dumont announced with a growl as he walked into Juliet Beaudreau's office.

"What happened?" Juliet hastily shifted a pile of papers to clear a chair for her unexpected visitor.

But Luc ignored the empty seat and paced instead, not easy to do in the tiny room that served as Juliet's office in the lowest level of the tower in St. Michel's de Bergeron Palace. Luc's very presence made the room seem even smaller. He was the kind of man who made an impression.

He'd certainly made an impression the first time Juliet had met him three years ago. Ever since then she always lit up inside whenever she saw him. Tall and lean, with thick brown hair and rakishly carved features, he had the most vivid blue eyes she'd ever seen. Instead of his usual work attire of a perfectly fitted black suit and light-blue shirt with a burgundy tie, he was wearing a black shirt and pants, which made her think he'd literally just returned to the palace from his most recent trip.

He was a man of many facets, deeply serious at times, wryly humorous at others. There had always been something slightly smoldering about him, deep beneath his cultured exterior.

At the moment he simply looked gorgeous...and upset.

"What happened?" Luc repeated. "You wouldn't believe me if I told you."

"Certainly I would. Did you finally find the lost heir?" She knew that as head of the country's Security Force, Luc had been assigned the mission of tracking down the missing heir to the throne of St. Michel.

"It looks as if I have." Luc kept pacing.

"You don't appear to be very pleased with the outcome," Juliet noted, coming around the solid oak table she used as a desk to perch on the front corner. While doing so, she briefly wished she was wearing something a little more attractive than a black top and skirt before refocusing her attention on Luc's news. "Who is it? We already know it's not Sebastian LeMarc. His claim proved to be false."

"That was his mother's doing, not his. Mothers can be a deceiving lot sometimes." Luc's voice held such bitterness.

Concerned, Juliet placed her hand on his arm, temporarily stopping his restless pacing. "Talk to me, Luc. Tell me what's going on. You know you can trust me."

It stung slightly that he didn't acknowledge her trustworthiness, but he did begin talking. "I just returned from visiting my father."

Which might explain his unsettled mood. Maybe it had to do with his family and not with the missing heir. "Did the visit go badly?"

"Depends on who you ask," Luc replied cryptically.

"What happened?"

"I have to fill you in on a bit of background first. My mother died when I was six," he said curtly, "and my father remarried after that."

"And your new stepmother was awful," Juliet continued. "And you were sent away to school in England, first to Eton and then to Cambridge."

Luc frowned. "How did you know that?"

Uh-oh. Juliet tried to backpedal. "Didn't you tell me?"

He shook his head. "No. I don't talk about my family life with anyone."

"All right," she reluctantly admitted. "I checked out your resumé, okay? Before he died, King Philippe granted me unlimited access to the royal archives and records."

"To do your thesis on the history of St. Michel, not to go nosing around in my personnel files. And I'm sure they didn't list anything about my stepmother being awful."

"I discerned that much for myself. Are you angry with me?" She gave him her most winning smile.

He wearily shook his head. "No. I'll let you off easy this time. Anyway, since I was sent off to school in England, my father and I haven't spent much time together. Maybe if we had, the lies would have come out sooner."

"What lies?"

"The lies about everything. About the man I thought was my father, the woman who was my mother, about the man I am today." His voice was rough with emotion.

Juliet had never seen Luc so upset. She didn't know if it was due to his English schooling or his work with Interpol before coming to St. Michel, but Luc was always a man in control, a man with hidden depths, a man who maintained his cool and kept his distance.

Juliet suspected it was because of his upbringing, that he had felt like an outsider in his own family once he was packed off to school. She knew the feeling well. As the late king's stepdaughter, she'd never really felt like part of the royal family. Her stepsisters, once the royal princesses, had never deliberately made her feel like an outcast. But she *was* different. She was the dark-haired, shy, bookish one amid all the pretty and popular blondes.

She'd always felt as if she didn't really belong. The one person who had befriended her was Luc. He might be thirty-two to her twenty-two, but she was older than her years. And she felt a special kind of bond with Luc, a bond she'd never dared explore for fear of ruining what they already had.

She knew Luc saw her only as a friend and that was fine, she'd take whatever she got. And she'd be the best darn friend Luc had ever had.

"Whatever lies might involve your father or your mother, I can tell you one thing about the man you are today," Juliet fiercely said. "You're an honorable man."

"You don't know what it's like, finding out your entire life is based on a lie."

"And I'm not likely to know what it's like if you don't tell me exactly what happened." Now her voice was tinged with a bit of exasperation.

"I'm not making much sense am I?" he noted wryly.

"No, but that's okay. Why don't you start at the beginning and go from there?"

"Ah, the beginning. Well, that would be with Prince Philippe's marriage to Katie, the one the young prince was told was invalid because Katie was underage at seventeen."

"Yes, but we know now that that wasn't true," Juliet reminded him. "The marriage *was* legal and valid. That's why you've been searching for their child all these months.''

"Yes, well, the search is over.''

"And you're having a bad heir day. That's what you said when you came in. And I'm assuming that you were referring to the missing heir, not to a haircut gone wrong.''

Luc had wonderfully thick brown hair. At the moment it had an unusually rumpled look about it, due to his shoving impatient fingers through it. "You assume correctly. I was referring to the missing heir.''

"And you still haven't told me who he is.''

"I know. It's just I'm finding this entire thing a little hard to accept.''

"What entire thing?''

"Well, finding out that my father isn't really my father at all for one thing.''

Her exasperation instantly melted away. "Oh, Luc.''

He tried to shrug it off, but she could tell he was more disturbed than he was letting on.

"My life is turning into one of those American soap operas,'' he growled in disgust.

"Did your father tell you this news while you were visiting him?''

"No. I went to see him to get to the bottom of this mess.''

She was confused. "What mess?''

"I had reason to believe that Albert Dumont might not be my real father. He confirmed it. My mother was married before. And not just once, but twice.''

"Did Albert know who your father is?''

"He didn't know at the time, no. All he knew was that my mother was unhappy with Robert Johnson, her previous husband, and that she divorced him. Apparently the lout cheated on her. Albert did business with the corporation Robert Johnson worked for, and he met my mother at some official function. Albert was also divorced and once my mother was free, the two of them married and settled down in France. I was all of two or three at the time. I know my mother's father died shortly thereafter, leaving her with no relatives in America.''

"So Albert thought that you were this Robert Johnson's child?''

"Well, apparently not. Apparently Albert knew that my mother was pregnant with another man's child when she married Robert. She asked Albert to let me believe Albert was my father, even going so far as to arrange for a fake French birth certificate for Luc Dumont, listing Albert as my father and Katherine as my mother.''

Juliet could see why he felt betrayed. The man he thought was his father turned out not to be his father after all. So many lies.

His voice was harsh. "Luc Dumont doesn't really exist.''

"Of course you do. I'm looking at you, pacing my office like a caged lion.''

"Why did you have to set up shop down here anyway?'' He dropped onto the empty chair and fixed her with an aggravated glare. "We could have found you a bigger office in the north wing.''

"I love it here.'' She waved a hand at her small but cozy surroundings. The grey stone walls dated back to the 16th century, their irregular surface still showing the marks where they'd been chiseled by hand. Aside from the oak table she'd retrieved from the royal storage room, she had a pair of mismatched Chippendale chairs, a mahogany bookcase and a lady's Victorian chintz armchair all squeezed into the tiny space. A tattered Oriental rug covered the stone floor. "You can see the gardens right outside my window."

She paused a second to enjoy the climbing pink roses that grew along the tower walls, framing her view of brilliant-colored flowering shrubs beyond, including luscious rhododendron and some late-blooming azaleas, graced by a trio of white butterflies dancing in the air. In the distance were the beds of sweet-smelling peonies and vibrant poppies and irises in colors ranging from deep purple to palest white.

She never tired of looking outside and drinking in the natural beauty. It fed her soul. Not that she'd ever tell anyone that. They already thought she was a little strange, a bookish oddity.

"The tower is one of the oldest parts of the palace," she continued. "Since I'm researching the history of St. Michel for my postgraduate work, this is the perfect place for me."

"Close enough to the boiler room that you can hear the pipes clang in the winter."

"True, but it's spring now. And you're trying to sidetrack me." She returned her gaze to him. "It won't work, you know. I have a one-track mind. It's why I'm so good with research. Once I get an idea into my head, I carry it through. So let's get back to you and your family. You said earlier that it all started with Prince Philippe's wedding to Katie. How so? Did Katie know your mother?"

"You don't understand. Katie *was* my mother."

Juliet was stunned. "But...but..." she sputtered. "That would make you..."

"The missing heir." Luc nodded. "Bingo. Now you see why I said I was having a bad heir day. Here I've been chasing all over Europe and America and it turns out *I'm* the missing heir. How ironic is that?"

She didn't know about ironic, but it was certainly freaking her out. She could only imagine how Luc must feel.

When he'd said that his father wasn't really his father, she'd never made the connection between his royal search and his family life. Luc had always been like her—an outsider to the inner circle of royalty, someone with regular rather than royal blood.

But not anymore. Now even that link between them was being broken.

"You're the missing heir," she repeated slowly. "Your father was…"

"King Philippe, who, when he was still a prince, married my mother Katherine, whom he called Katie. I should have made the connection." He was on his feet and pacing again. "I'm a trained investigator, for heaven's sake. But it never even occurred to me. She died when I was so young, I don't remember much about her. The only thing I have is a book on St. Michel she used to read to me. I kept it for sentimental value."

"Who else knows about this?"

"Sometimes it feels like everyone knew but me."

"What are you going to do?"

"How should I know? I'm still trying to absorb it all."

"Queen Celeste will not be pleased." Celeste was King Philippe's fourth and most recent wife, now widow. When King Philippe had died of a heart attack, the country had grieved, but those in power had panicked.

For one thing, according to ancient St. Michel law, the throne couldn't be passed to a female. And when the dowager queen had made her startling declaration that the king had married secretly at the age of eighteen and that a child had resulted…well, the palace had been turned upside down.

"Celeste is still maintaining that the child she's carrying is a boy," Juliet said.

"And I suppose she's still refusing to have an ultrasound to determine the baby's sex, right?" Luc asked.

Juliet nodded. "Correct."

"What a mess."

"You're the heir," she repeated. "The oldest male. The future king of St. Michel. I'm going to have to practice curtsying."

"You do and I won't speak to you," he warned her.

"But it's protocol to curtsy to the king."

"What do I know about being a king?"

"Well, for one thing, you're very good at giving orders," she pointed out with a grin.

"Sure. Orders are easy. Reporting what I just found to the prime minister and dowager queen, that is not going to be easy."

"Why not?"

"Who'd believe that I'm the future king?" Luc scoffed. "I'm not a diplomatic man. I don't know anything about governing."

"You can learn. I'm certain the prime minister and the dowager queen will be delighted with this news."

"I brought proof with me," he said abruptly. "Not so much to convince them as to convince myself. It seems my mother left a key to a safety deposit box in Albert's care, to use if I ever came asking about my birth father. Since I didn't know Albert wasn't my father, it was doubtful I'd ever think to ask him anything. Inside the box was a registered copy of my birth certificate. I thought it had to be another fake, but I checked the paper trail, this time using my mother's name and it checks out. Before that I was looking for Katie Graham, her name on the marriage certificate to Prince Philippe. I'd already traced Katie back to Texas and found she married Ellsworth Johnson.''

"I thought you said his name was Robert Johnson?"

"Americans have this irritating habit of not using their proper Christian given names, especially Texans. Robert was his middle name. It was all there in the safe deposit box. Marriage certificates, my birth certificate and a letter from my mother."

"Really? What did she say?"

"I haven't read it yet."

"Why not?"

"Because I don't know if I can forgive her," Luc said bluntly. "And I don't think there's anything she could have written in that letter that would justify her lying to me, or letting me live a lie."

"Maybe she was trying to protect you. She was so young when you were born. Barely eighteen. Pregnant and alone. She tried to provide you with a stable home and father when she married Albert."

"She married one man knowing she was pregnant with another man's child." A muscle flexed in his clenched jaw. "How honorable is that?"

"You won't know until you read her letter," she replied.

"I don't need to read it to know what she did was dishonorable."

"I realize you feel that way now, but you have to read her letter, Luc."

"If you're so interested, then you read it," he growled, yanking it out of his pocket and tossing it onto her book-strewn desk. "I'm not interested. I don't care what it says. Now if you'll excuse me, I have to prepare for my meeting with the prime minister and dowager queen and I need some fresh air to clear my head.''

With that curt announcement, Luc left as abruptly as he'd arrived.

CHAPTER

morning that the white mailtruck had crested down the
St. Paul roads from one...
Well, that can't go on forever now, can it? she spoke to
be

...

Chapter Two

Juliet stared down at the envelope on her desk as if it were a snake that might lunge out and bite her. Her fingers trembled as she traced the elegant handwriting— *Luc.*

What had his mother been thinking when she'd written his name? Had she hoped that he'd never find out he was heir to the throne of St. Michel? Would she even have known? From what Luc had told her of the investigation, Katie had been told that her marriage to Philippe was illegal.

Which meant Katie would have believed her son to be illegitimate. And she'd have done everything she could to hide that fact from him.

Juliet knew how much legitimacy mattered. The royal princesses had had to weather that storm of controversy themselves when Lise's rotten first husband Wilhelm had sold the story to a tabloid. Once the word was out that King Philippe had had a secret first wife, whom he'd never divorced, the paparazzi had swarmed the de Bergeron Palace like a bunch of locusts, feeding off the scandal.

The princesses had all left the palace now—Marie-Claire had married Sebastian, Ariane had gone to Rhineland and married Prince Etienne, Lise had finally found true happiness with her former brother-in-law, the honorable Charles Rodin. Juliet's own half sister Jacqueline was visiting cousins in Switzerland and protected from most of the scandal while their brother Georges had headed off to the Andes in Peru for a few weeks of summer skiing.

At least things had worked out well in the end for the three older princesses, who had all found the men of their dreams.

Juliet thought she'd found the man of her dreams as well—Luc. Her chances of having him see her in a romantic way had always been slim at best, but now they were impossible.

Juliet turned and caught her reflection in the small mirror propped on top of the bookcase along the opposite wall. She'd placed it there to reflect the view of the garden rather than out of any vanity on her part.

She had nothing to be vain about. Her green eyes were all right, she supposed, but her long dark hair had never behaved properly, and was at this moment falling out of the topknot she'd secured it in with a pencil to hold it in place. Her eyebrows were bushy, or so her roommate in boarding school had once told her, and her mouth was too large to be elegant. She even had freckles, something no princess would ever have.

Of course, she wasn't a princess. She was the ugly stepsister. The smart one, the bookworm, more interested in the past than in her future.

On those occasions lately when she had dreamt about

her future, she'd placed Luc at her side. Her gaze traveled from her reflection to the letter on her desk.

The fact that Luc was the missing heir changed *everything*.

She certainly didn't have what it took to make a king happy. She didn't even have what it took to keep a rich St. Michel businessman's son like Armand Killey happy. Three years ago, Armand had swept her off her feet, telling her he loved her quiet beauty. And she'd bought every word, had, in fact, hungered for someone to love her after her mother had died.

But Armand hadn't really loved her at all. He'd simply been using her in order to get close to the king. Juliet had heard him and his father discussing the plan. She'd been devastated and humiliated, as well as angry with herself for being so stupid as to fall for Armand's slick ways in the first place.

"Did you read the letter yet?" Luc asked, disrupting her thoughts and once again catching her unprepared. He must have gotten the fresh air he'd said he needed by taking a brief walk in the garden, out of her line of vision.

"No." She paused to remove the pencil from her hair and let the dark strands tumble where they may. She'd learned long ago there was no fighting her hair, it always won. If it didn't want to stay up, it wouldn't. Turning to face Luc, she said, "I did not read it. And I'm not going to until you do."

"Then you'll be waiting a very long time," he retorted, "since I have no intention of ever reading it."

"Luc." She reached out to cover his hand with hers. "You're upset right now. Don't make any decisions just yet."

"Don't make any decisions?" His voice was harsh, making him sound like a man pushed to his limits as he pulled his hand away. "I have to. I have to tell the prime minister and the dowager queen what I've discovered. I have an appointment with them both in less than half an hour."

Juliet tried not to be hurt by his physical withdrawal from her, reminding herself that he had a lot to deal with. A good friend wouldn't get all sensitive, wouldn't show her pain. She'd be supportive and reassuring. "As I said before, I'm sure they will be pleased with the news."

"And as *I* said before, I know nothing about being a king."

"There is a silver lining in all this you know. At least you won't have to worry about getting along with the new king."

"Trust you to find a silver lining."

She wrinkled her nose at him. "You make me sound like a naive Pollyanna who still believes in happy endings."

"You don't believe in happy endings?"

"My mother never found her happy ending," Juliet noted somberly. "She married Philippe out of a sense of duty, hoping to provide for her children, Georges and I. I don't think she ever truly loved the king the way she loved my father. Which was perhaps a good thing given the fact that the king only wanted one thing from my mother—an heir. In the end she died trying to provide him a son."

"Are you bitter about that?"

His question surprised her. "I try not to let myself be, but it is difficult at times," she admitted. "After the first baby was stillborn, the doctors warned that another pregnancy might be risky. But the king wouldn't listen and my mother went along with his wishes. Jacqueline was born a year later. I think the fact that the pregnancy went so well lulled the king and my mother into a false sense of security. Two years later my mother was pregnant again. This time things did not go as well." Juliet's throat tightened as it always did when she thought of those dark days. "I miss her still. That's why I feel so strongly about you reading this letter from your mother, Luc. Because I know the influence a mother can have, and how that loss leaves a void in you."

"My situation is entirely different. My mother died when I was six. I don't remember much about her."

"Perhaps reading her letter will bring back some memories."

"I don't want to remember," Luc stated bluntly, returning to his earlier pacing. "I've got enough trouble dealing with the present without dredging up the past any more than I absolutely have to. As it is, I'll have to rehash the entire story for the prime minister and dowager queen."

"The dowager queen has always had a soft spot in her heart for you."

"She just has an eye for younger men."

"Luc!" Juliet gave him a startled look before laughing somewhat guiltily. "You shouldn't say such things."

"See, I told you I'm not cut out to be king. Already I'm saying the wrong thing." His words sounded serious but there was a slight twinkle in his eyes.

"Well, the dowager queen is your grandmother so I suppose one could say something slightly outrageous about one's own grandmother."

"My grandmother?" Now Luc was the one who looked startled. "I hadn't thought about that."

"And with Marie-Claire, Ariane, Lise and Jacqueline, you've got four sisters."

"Half sisters," he corrected her. "Three of whom

have all married in the past few months. There must be something in the palace water that's responsible for all these weddings.''

"Your half sisters would disagree with you, I'm sure. They all married for love."

"A romantic idea to be sure," he scoffed.

"You don't believe in marrying for love?"

"It isn't something kings are supposed to do, is it?" Luc replied, pausing in front of her desk to bestow a brooding look down at the letter still resting there. "Supposedly King Philippe and my mother were in love, and look where it got them. It seems to have messed up the rest of their lives."

"It doesn't have to happen that way."

"Oh, so now you're the expert on royal love, hmm?" He turned to face her, propping his hip on the corner of the oak table as she had earlier. "I thought your thesis was on the role royal women played in St. Michel's history."

"And that role sometimes included falling in love."

"What about you? Have you ever fallen in love?" Luc asked her.

"I thought so at the time." Then Luc had come to the palace and things had changed. Her feelings for Armand had dimmed in comparison to her awareness of Luc. "What about you?"

"Love makes you vulnerable and I try not to be vulnerable."

No surprise there. "If you're so invulnerable," she teased him, "then you shouldn't be nervous about this upcoming meeting with the prime minister. You should be cool and calm, as you always are. A man in control."

"Is that how you see me?"

She nodded. It was easier than adding that it was one

of the ways she saw him, that she also sensed something deeper within him.

"Well, I'll take that as a compliment then. Doesn't stop me from being uneasy about this meeting, however."

"Do you want me to help..." Juliet began, before stopping as she remembered that it was the king, not merely Luc, she was offering assistance to. As if a king would need a bookworm's help. "Never mind." She took a step away from him.

"No, go ahead. You were going to offer help with what?"

"Your meeting. By coming with you. A stupid idea."

"Not stupid at all. You've got a quiet way of getting people on your side. But this is one battle I've got to fight on my own."

"Of course," she said formally, taking another step back. "I understand and I agree."

"Why are you doing that?" Luc demanded, noting the change in her voice immediately.

"Doing what?"

"Going all proper and starchy on me, pulling away from me."

"This office isn't large enough for me to move very far away," she pointed out in an attempt to add a little levity.

But Luc wasn't buying her act for one second. Giving her a dark look, he said, "Don't you dare start acting differently now that you know about me being..." He paused and sliced the air with his hand instead of continuing.

"King," Juliet said. "The word you are searching for is *king*. And you can't expect me to act as if nothing has happened."

"I expect you to continue to be my friend as you've been since I arrived at the palace three years ago."

"I will always be your friend, Luc, but this is bound to change things between us."

"Not if we don't let it. And I refuse to let it," he stated. "You must promise to do the same."

She shook her head. "I don't think I can promise that."

"Why not?"

"Because you being the king changes everything. Some things we have no control over."

"The one thing I plan on doing with this situation is maintaining control," Luc stated firmly.

"Some things are beyond our control," she repeated with soft sadness.

Some things…like falling in love with a man who would be king.

"So Luc, I hope the fact that you called this special meeting means you have some good news to report to us," Prime Minister René Davoine said with his customary dignity. Slim and blessed with plenty of pewter-gray hair and a mustache to match, he was the picture of a distinguished statesman. Dressed in a two-piece dark suit as always, he appeared more somber than he actually was.

"I have news, but I'm not certain how good it is," Luc replied.

"Don't mutter, Luc," Dowager Queen Simone instructed him tartly.

Standing before the two of them made him feel like a bug under a microscope. As for the dowager queen, he'd never met anyone quite like her.

Thin and regal, she possessed a presence that filled the

room—and considering they were in the huge Throne Room, that was no small feat. At age seventy-five, she had her short dark hair meticulously maintained so that not one hint of gray or white showed.

Aside from her attitude, her eyes were the most memorable thing about her. They were a piercing blue, not as dark as his own, more the color of a light sabre. They certainly had a way of slicing right through a person who irritated her, which he'd apparently just done.

Queen Celeste had tried to convince anyone who would listen that Dowager Queen Simone was "dotty." And, while the older monarch had forgotten some details of the events that surrounded her son's early marriage, there was no denying that in most cases the dowager queen was still as sharp as a tack.

She was eyeing him with honed intensity. "Those English schools taught you how to enunciate properly."

"I could speak in French or German or Italian, if you prefer, ma'am," Luc retorted.

She waved his words away with an imperious wave of her wrinkled but still elegant hand. On her left hand was the elaborate diamond ring that her husband, King Antoine, had given her upon their engagement over fifty years ago. She'd outlived both her husband and her only son due not only to her strong constitution but also to her iron will. "English will suffice."

"Please be seated, Luc," the prime minister said with a much more inviting wave of his hand.

Luc sat on the Louis XIV chair as if it might collapse beneath him. This sudden attack of nerves was so unlike him. He'd been dealing with the prime minister and the dowager queen for months without any problem. But that had been when he'd been an employee, when he'd been head of the country's Security Force. It was a job he enjoyed, a job he knew how to do, a job he was very good at.

Damn. He should have asked Juliet to come with him when she'd offered. She'd know what to say. While she was shy around large groups of strangers, she had a way of disarming people with her quiet smile and sincere empathy.

"Well, Luc?" The prime minister looked at him encouragingly. "Have you found the missing heir?"

"I believe so, yes."

"You *believe* so?" Simone said. "You mean there is some room for doubt?"

"No. I found the birth certificate for Katie Graham's child, a son."

"A son." The prime minister almost applauded with delight. "Have you located him?"

"Yes."

"I told you Luc would succeed," the prime minister said.

"What is this son like? Is he someone suitable? He's not living in some American trailer park, is he?" Dowager Queen Simone demanded. "Someone who would be a disgrace to the throne and the de Bergeron name?"

"I don't believe he'd be a disgrace, no," Luc replied. "Naturally he's somewhat stunned with the news."

The dowager queen leaned forward eagerly, her thin hands resting on her gold-filigree-topped cane. "Where is he?"

"You're looking at him."

She blinked her laser eyes at him. "I don't understand."

"Katie Graham was my mother."

Luc could relate to the look of astonishment on the

prime minister's face. He'd felt that way himself when he'd first heard the news. He *still* felt that way.

The dowager queen's expression was harder to read.

"If you knew Katie Graham was your mother, then why on earth did you spend the past few months searching for her son?" the prime minister asked.

"I knew my mother as Katherine Dumont," Luc replied. "I had no idea about her...colorful past. It was only as I began the investigation that I started putting the pieces together. Even then, I didn't believe it could really be true. When I went to my father—the man I believed to be my father—and confronted him, he gave me the key to a safe deposit box that my mother had requested I open should I ever question my heritage. It's all here." He opened the manilla envelope he'd brought with him. "The entire paper trail—wedding certificate, my real birth certificate, not the one my mother had Albert Dumont falsify."

"Falsified birth certificates seem to have reached epidemic proportions around here lately," Simone noted tartly.

Luc flinched.

"Not that we're accusing you of any such behavior," the prime minister hurriedly assured him.

"I can understand your skepticism," Luc said. "I considered not sharing this information with you at all, just pretending I never found it."

"Why would you do something like that?" the prime minister asked.

"Because I'm not any happier about this...situation than you are," Luc said in a clipped voice.

"You misunderstand me." Simone put her thin hand on his arm. He was surprised to feel it trembling slightly. "Is it really possible? Could you be...my grandson?"

"According to those papers I am. Even so, I'd still like to get corroborating evidence from an independent source before we proceed any further."

"You sound as if you're not happy with this news, Luc," the prime minister said. "I can tell you that I, for one, cannot think of a more honorable man to take the throne."

Simone was looking almost gleeful. "You know what this means? It means that awful Celeste won't get her grasping hands on the throne. Her baby is due any minute now, and if it's a boy, well, then our ship would have been sunk."

"I don't think Queen Celeste will take the news about Luc very well," the prime minister noted.

"As I said," Luc interrupted them. "No one but the three of us and Juliet is to know about this news just yet."

"Juliet?" Simone raised a perfectly penciled eyebrow. "So you told Juliet. Before you told us?"

Luc refused to squirm in his seat. He was a former Interpol agent, he was not a schoolboy being reprimanded by his headmaster.

"Yes, I told Juliet before I told you." The set of his jaw communicated his aggravation. "Do you have a problem with that?"

"I fear it would do me no good if I did," Simone replied. "I've always liked Juliet. She's a wise little thing. So what did she advise you to do?"

"She didn't advise, she listened." Luc's pointed look indicated it was something that the older woman could learn to do better.

Simone smiled and leaned back in her chair with satisfaction. "Yes, you will do well as the king. Quite well indeed."

"I want you both to swear you won't tell anyone about this information until we can get it confirmed," Luc said. "And the situation with Rhineland also has to be addressed."

The prime minister paused in his close inspection of the material Luc had handed him. "The birth certificate is registered, and the rest of the documents appear legitimate."

"I know someone from Interpol, someone very discreet, who will do some follow-up work," Luc said.

"I understand you were born in Texas," Simone said with a slight shudder. "Thank goodness Katie had the foresight to bring you back to Europe and civilization. Imagine if we'd had to track you down in Texas, as some kind of roving cowboy."

"You've been watching too many movies," Luc said. "Not everyone in Texas is a cowboy." He knew, he'd traveled to Texas during the course of his investigation.

"Some are ruthless businessmen like J. R. Ewing," the dowager queen continued, "on that television show…what was it called? 'Houston'?"

"'Dallas'," Luc corrected her.

"There's no point in worrying over what might have been," the prime minister said. "We should focus on what our next course of action should be. I will need to notify the Privy Council."

"I'm still trying to get information from the French customs agency about Katie Graham's arrival and departure from France. Those records from over thirty years ago are in some warehouse waiting to be transferred onto the computer system."

"What do you hope to gain from those records?" the prime minister asked.

"The date Katie arrived in France to marry King Philippe and the date she left for the United States," Luc said.

"But you already have so much information from earlier in your investigation," the prime minister noted, opening his own file on the subject. "The marriage certificate between Katie and Philippe, the birth certificate of her son Lucas Johnson, the marriage certificate of Katie Graham and Ellsworth Johnson, the divorce certificate of Katie Graham and said Mr. Johnson and lastly her marriage certificate to Albert Dumont."

"I could still be Albert's son, just trying to pass myself off as the king's."

"DNA testing would resolve that." The prime minister gazed over the top edge of his reading glasses before removing them entirely to solemnly ask Luc, "Would you be willing to subject yourself to that?"

Luc paused before nodding.

"Ah," Simone murmured. "I understand now. It is not that you want us to be sure you are the real heir, it is that you yourself are not sure that you *want* to be the king. Isn't that correct, Luc?"

Yes, Luc silently noted, the elderly dowager queen was still sharp as a tack, all right. She'd certainly summed up his emotions in no time at all.

"Your Majesty?" the footman whispered to Celeste as he delivered her lunch to her suite on the second floor of the palace. "I have some information for you."

Shortly after her marriage Celeste had completely redecorated the suite in shades of ivory and gold. She thought the colors complemented her own coloring—the ivory of her flawless skin, the gold of her perfectly cut hair.

"Information? It had better be something good," she

warned him. "The baby has been kicking me all day and I'm not in the best of moods, Henri."

"I overheard a conversation…"

"Overheard?"

"I was clearing the dowager queen's tea tray from the Ruby Salon, which is right beside the Throne Room."

"I am aware of the location of the rooms in this palace," Celeste said. "Get on with it."

"I happened to be standing next to the closed doorway leading into the Throne Room and happened to overhear the conversation between the prime minister, the dowager queen and Luc Dumont."

"Luc is back from France?"

"He arrived this very afternoon."

"With news I presume?"

"Yes, ma'am. Outrageous news."

"Well hurry and tell me, I haven't got all day. I believe I've gone into labor." Celeste gripped the front of the footman's ornate jacket. "Tell me…and quickly!"

"Luc is claiming that he is the rightful heir."

Celeste's grip on the footman tightened until she was almost choking the small man.

"Of course, I do not believe it," the footman wheezed, struggling for air. "You are our most beloved and beautiful queen."

"And I'm about to give birth to a boy," she said, panting slightly. "A boy who will be the king. Go now. Fetch Dr. Mellion. Get him and no one else. You understand?"

Henri nodded so fast his footman's cap almost fell off.

"And tell no one what you have heard about Luc," Celeste continued. "It is all a lie, a conspiracy by that dotty old woman and her crazy prime minister. Remember, Henri—" she released her grip on him and patted his arm as she smiled her famously charming smile ''—I will reward those who are loyal to me. Reward them *greatly*.''

"Thank you, Your Majesty. My only aim is to serve you.''

Her smile slipped as another contraction hit. "Then go get Dr. Mellion and be quick about it!''

Chapter Three

"Have you heard the news?" Juliet asked Luc the next morning. She'd come to his office first thing. They were alone, and with the office door closed, assured of some privacy.

Unlike her own working space, his was spacious and possessed every modern convenience—computer, fax machine, a bank of telephones. His desk held a blotter, a penholder and a lamp. No mess, no pile of papers. Everything was neatly in its place, under control. Even the chairs in his office possessed a firm practicality that didn't make them particularly nice to sit in, but she plopped into the nearest one anyway.

"What news?" Luc barely looked up from the file he was studying.

"Celeste had a baby boy at four this morning."

"Oh, that news," he said absently. "Yes, I heard."

He'd reverted back to his usual working attire of a perfectly-fitted black suit and light blue shirt with a burgundy tie. He looked very classy...and very much like a "hottie" to quote her sister Jacqueline's favorite terminology.

Wishing she could just sit here and admire the view—him—Juliet realized she should try to keep her mind on court business and not funny business, like making out with Luc on his smooth desktop. "Did you hear she's proclaiming he's the next King of St. Michel?"

"Celeste has proclaimed a number of things over the past few months. It doesn't mean any of them are true."

Too jumpy to sit still for long, Juliet abandoned the chair for the corner of his desk, where she perched. Luc clearly hadn't noticed the flowing floral skirt she was wearing, nor the gauzy pink camisole top that had required all her nerve to put on. After all, she *was* visiting the future king. She'd almost put on the nunnish gray dress she wore to chapel. But some spark of rebellion had prompted her to stick to her present attire. "Did you tell her that you're the real heir to the throne?"

"No." Luc closed the file he'd been studying. "She was rather busy last night."

"When do you plan on telling her?"

Getting up to come around his desk and join her on the front edge of the desk, Luc replied, "As late as possible."

Juliet nodded understandingly. "She's not going to be pleased."

"Now there's an understatement," he noted dryly.

"When is the announcement going to be made about you being the true heir? How did the dowager queen and prime minister take the news? And…"

"One question at a time." Luc placed a teasing finger over her lips, effectively silencing her questions while sending her heart into overdrive. His skin was warm against hers. She was suddenly assailed with the urge to draw his finger into her mouth, to taste his skin.

She leapt away as if burned, almost falling from the desk. What kind of wanton was she to have such thoughts? Especially about the future king! She should never have worn this camisole top. It gave a girl ideas, ideas that she was far sexier than she really was, far more confident.

"Something wrong?" Luc asked.

She frantically shook her head, her dark hair tumbling down into her eyes. A pencil wasn't the best hairclip, but it's what she usually used to wrap her hair up into a knot on top of her head, and she'd somehow misplaced all of hers, which wasn't surprising. She often got so engrossed with her research that she lost track of things like pencils. So she'd had to leave her hair loose this morning.

"No, nothing." She wanted to sit down, but now felt awkward doing so while he still stood. All of a sudden the realization that he was the king was overshadowing *everything* else. "Go on with what you were saying, please. I didn't mean to interrupt."

"I don't care if you interrupt."

"It isn't polite."

"Which brings me to my next topic."

He still hadn't answered her previous questions, but she wasn't about to point that out now. Instead she tried to look properly attentive and respectful and not as if she secretly longed to kiss him.

"I want you to do a favor for me," Luc said.

"I'll do whatever I can."

He smiled. "I was hoping you'd say that. Because I want you to give me royalty training."

She stared at him blankly. "Excuse me?"

"I want you to teach me all the kingly things I'll need to know."

When she just blinked owlishly at him, he put it another way. "I'd like you to tutor me on protocol, customs and traditions of the royal family."

"I'm sure the protocol minister would be glad to help…"

Luc cut off her words. "No way am I going to that toady fellow. I dealt with him when I first arrived at the palace and he had the effrontery to tell me not to chew gum in front of the king. What are you smiling at?"

"Your use of the word *effrontery*. A very regal term."

"I don't feel regal," he confessed. "It feels so strange to think of King Philippe as my…father."

"I imagine it does. I know none of this has been easy for you."

"And it's not going to get any easier. Which is why I need you to help me quickly learn my way about. You and no one else."

If only that were true. If only he did need her, as a woman rather than as a friend. And if only he wasn't the future king. And if only she were more beautiful and confident. And had bigger breasts. Hey, since she was making wishes here, she might as well wish for the entire package.

"So what do you say?" Luc asked.

"I'm honored that you'd ask me, but I truly don't feel I'm the best person for this job."

"I feel you are."

"There, you're already sounding like a king. You don't need me."

"You're doing it again," he warned her.

"Doing what?"

"Going all strange on me. All distant."

"I'm sorry if I've offended you."

"Oh please." He rolled his eyes at her. "You used to take great joy in offending me."

"I did not!" she vehemently denied. "Name one time when I did that."

"When I told you that men made better leaders than women and you said I was sounding like a chauvinist pig."

"Well, you were. But that was before…"

"I want the two of us to remain as we were before."

Which was part of the problem. He was happy with them just being friends as they'd been before, whereas she wanted so much more. And now those hopes were futile. As king, Luc had to marry someone worthy, someone who had the confidence and polish of the royal princesses, not an ugly duckling like herself. And she knew herself well enough to know that the more time she spent with Luc, the more intense her emotions for him were likely to get. Not a smart thing. And if nothing else, she was a smart woman.

"Come on, Juliet, I can't do this without you."

He could, of course. She knew he could. But it was impossible for her to turn away from the look of teasing pleading in his intense blue eyes. She doubted there were many women on the entire planet who could turn Luc down when he gave them that look—no matter what he wanted.

"Protocol and traditions, right?" she said briskly.

"Right. Piece of cake, right?"

"Speaking of cake, I think we'll begin with royal meals and formal state dinners." She kept her voice coolly efficient. If she was going to be coerced into doing this, she was going to do it her way.

"That sounds fine. There's just one thing. I don't want anyone knowing you're giving me these lessons."

"Why?" Was he ashamed of being seen with her? The thought stung like a cruel barb.

"Why? Because I don't want anyone else knowing yet about my being the future king," he explained. "Not until the corroborating documentation comes in. I figure we have about a week to ten days before that happens."

"So you're not telling Celeste that you're the king until then?"

"That's right. I thought you and I could get together later at night, after everyone else in the palace has gone to bed," Luc suggested. "Would that work for you?"

Work for her? None of this worked for her. Not one single thing. Not him thinking of her as a friend, not him being king, certainly not her spending more time alone with him. But there was no changing reality. And the reality was that she had to help him. "That will be fine." She could only hope that stating it so confidently would make it so.

Bond. Juliet Bond. That's how she felt. As if she were participating in some sort of covert operation.

She was even wearing the appropriate clothing—black, so she wouldn't be seen in the palace's shadowy hallways. King Philippe had ordered a reduction in the electricity used within the palace, and had replaced the light bulbs with low-wattage models that wouldn't need replacing for a decade.

The dim light served her purposes well. So did the fact that most of the servants had gone home to their own beds in St. Michel, leaving only a skeletal staff behind in the palace. A hundred years ago, the staff would have lived on the top floor in the servants' quarters. But things had changed a lot in the past century.

She tried to imagine any of the royal women she was researching sneaking down the hallway toward the Crystal Ballroom to meet the future king. Only one kind of woman did that. A royal mistress. Not that a royal mistress would ever have been caught dead wearing the tailored black slacks and black long-sleeved T-shirt she was presently wearing. Or rubber-soled shoes so her footsteps would be quiet in the marble corridors. Not the sexiest of outfits.

As often happened, Juliet was so caught up in her own thoughts she didn't realize anyone was in front of her until she almost ran smack into him.

At least she didn't shriek in surprise. Instead she emitted a startled *oomph.*

A pair of male arms circled her waist. But even before they did so, she knew it was Luc. Her nose was buried in his shirtfront and she could smell the citrus scent of his soap.

He, too, had changed from his normal working attire. Instead he was wearing the most deliciously silky shirt in a midnight blue that brought out the color of his eyes. She noticed that the minute she looked up. She also noticed the fact that he was smiling at her. Little crinkles appeared at the corners of his eyes.

She'd once spent several hours trying to pinpoint the exact blue of his eyes. She'd even gone so far as to check out a color chart in an old watercolor set from her boarding school days.

She'd been younger then. And foolish.

Foolish enough to believe a man like him might come to have feelings for a girl like her. But now the man was about to become a king, leaving her even further behind.

"Nice outfit," Luc was saying with a grin. "All you need is some face camouflage and you'd be ready for a covert op."

"Since there are no jungles in St. Michel or in the palace, I didn't see the point in wearing camouflage. It's not as though we were rendezvousing in the Palm Room," she noted tartly, not appreciating his comments about her clothes.

"I'd never find you in all those palms and ferns in there. Besides, it's too easy for someone to spy on us."

"Now who's sounding like James Bond?" she countered mockingly.

"I already told you that I don't want anyone else knowing about our meetings."

"And I still say you'd be better off having the protocol minister assist you in this matter."

"Now don't go getting all prissy on me, it's not that I'm ashamed to be seen with you or anything. That's not what you're thinking, is it?" Luc demanded, studying her face. "Because you're dead wrong."

"If you say so, your majesty."

He glared at her. "None of that fancy talk."

"You're going to have to get used to it," she firmly informed him. "So you might as well start now."

"Not with you."

"Yes, with me. At any official function, you're going to have to be comfortable with the way others treat you. And they *will* treat you differently. You must learn to be comfortable with that."

"Or learn to be a damn good actor," he muttered.

"Which will no doubt come in handy as well," she briskly agreed. "Now, one of the royal rules is that no one is to speak to you unless spoken to. I can foresee that this will be a problem since you're so close-mouthed.''

"I am not closemouthed. See?" He pursed his open lips at her.

She was immediately distracted by his actions and by the sensual outline of his mouth—the sculpted curve of his upper lip, the seductive fullness of his lower one. There was little doubt that most women would be fascinated by his smile, fascinated by *him*…period. Even without the title of king. Without any title at all. Without *anything* at all.

Oh my. She raised her hands to her cheeks. Concentrate, she fiercely ordered herself. And not on him! On protocol. Which certainly precluded her having fantasies about him. *Focus on protocol. What were you saying? Oh yes, you were telling him that he was closemouthed, no, don't look at his lips again. Stay focused.*

"You must learn to speak first and initiate a conversation," she continued as if nothing had happened. "Go ahead. Pretend I've just walked into the royal dining room for an official function. What do you say?"

"Whaaatsuuup?" he drawled, like those American beer commercials they saw on satellite television.

She stifled a laugh and attempted to give him a reprimanding look worthy of Mrs. Friesen, the headmistress at her boarding school. Mrs. Friesen was the queen of reprimanding looks.

He lifted a brow. "What's wrong? Not appropriate?"

"Not appropriate," she agreed.

"Do I know you in this scenario? Are you an old friend or someone I've never seen before?"

"You don't know me," Juliet replied.

"Are you from St. Michel?" Luc asked.

"No."

"Then I'd ask you who were, where you're from, what you're doing in St. Michel... Now what's wrong?" he demanded as she sighed and shook her head.

"I said to initiate a conversation, not to interrogate me."

He arched one dark brow at her. "There's a difference?"

"Yes, there's a difference."

"You're talking to a man who spent eight years in Interpol before coming here to be Head of Security. I'm much better at interrogations than I am at conversations."

"You don't seem to have that trouble with me," Juliet pointed out. "You and I have had some wonderful conversations."

"You're different."

She wanted to ask him how she was different, but he answered before she could do so.

"You're a friend," Luc said.

As she'd suspected. She knew he only saw her as a friend and nothing more than that. *Get used to it and get over it.*

"How would you speak to a stranger?" she said.

"The way I just told you."

Juliet sighed. Changing his many years of Interpol training was clearly not going to happen overnight. "All right, we'll come back to conversation later. For now, let's concentrate on royal protocol. As our monarch, you and the highest-ranking foreign dignitary will walk into the dining room together. Your respective spouses will walk behind you."

"So which role are you playing?"

"Excuse me?"

"Are you the foreign dignitary or my spouse?"

While the thought of being Luc's spouse made her

insides melt, the thought of being the king's spouse made her stomach clench. "I'm a foreign dignitary."

"Fine. That means you walk into the room beside me, right?"

She nodded.

"Should I offer you my arm?" Luc asked.

"That's not necessary, no." She didn't want him touching her any more than was absolutely required. Which should be no touching at all.

"It's a little dark in here, isn't it?" Luc noted as they entered farther into the large room.

Juliet reached over to turn on the switch controlling the porcelain hand-painted chandelier. While nowhere near as grand as any of the ones in the Crystal Ballroom, this exquisite one-of-a-kind piece had been a gift from Queen Victoria. But the main focus in the room, aside from the series of Rembrandts hanging on the wall, was the huge table that seated forty easily.

She gestured for him to sit at the table before taking the seat beside him. "Normally the footmen would take care of our chairs, pulling them out and pushing them back in. As you can see, earlier this afternoon I laid out two place settings as if this were a formal dinner."

"There's enough silverware here to choke a horse."

"As the king, you shouldn't say anything about choking a horse," she chastised him. "It could be taken out of context and spread around the tabloids. Next thing you know, you're being portrayed as someone who is cruel to animals. You can ride, can't you?"

"Excuse me?"

"A horse. You can ride a horse, can't you?"

"Yes, although I haven't ridden a lot in the past year or so."

"Then we should stop by the stable for a brush-up

lesson. But back to the dinner. You probably attended some formal functions while you were at Cambridge.''

''Not really, no. As a university student, I drank a lot of Guinness and ate a lot of curry, the hotter the better.''

''Really? Why?''

He shrugged a little self-consciously. ''It's a macho thing.''

The idea of Luc trying to prove his machismo brought to mind more forbidden images of decidedly sensual ways in which he could demonstrate his manhood. Images filled her mind of wickedly tempting options that had him plying her with kisses hotter than any curry. That made her nervous, and, as she did whenever she was nervous, she started talking. ''Usually royals stay away from spicy things.'' She almost tripped over her own tongue as another chapter of images flashed into her mind—Luc and spicy things. Luc *as* a spicy thing. ''Um, I heard that garlic, spaghetti, tomato sauce and shellfish have been banned from the menu when the Queen of England pays an official visit to Italy. And the media has an unwritten rule never to photograph or film her while she's eating. The press has a similar rule here. Blackberries and summer raspberries are also off most royal menus, since having tiny seeds stuck in one's teeth would disfigure a royal smile. Fish and meat are served without bones to avoid a possible choking hazard, as once befell our dowager queen in her younger days. A similar incident occurred with the Queen Mum, Queen Elizabeth's mother, I believe.''

''How do you know all these things?''

''I was babbling, wasn't I? Sorry about that.'' She gave him a sheepish smile. ''My brother Georges often teases me that I'm nothing but a walking encyclopedia of trivia.''

"You're much more than an encyclopedia," Luc noted quietly.

He looked at her, meeting her gaze with a speculative interest that was a bit disconcerting. Her lashes tumbled over her eyes as she quickly shifted her eyes downward to the table.

"Yes, well..." She cleared her throat. "So you're saying that while you were at Cambridge you didn't attend any formal functions of any kind?"

"Only one—the graduation ceremony, filled with pomp and circumstance and traditional robes."

"Well, there you go then. That sounds very regal."

"That was over a decade ago."

"It's probably like riding a bike, once learned not forgotten."

"Aren't you going to ask me if I know how to ride a bike?"

"Bike-riding isn't an often-used activity for a royal."

"I biked a lot when I was in university."

She tried to imagine Luc on a bicycle, but kept seeing him on a big powerful motorbike instead. He'd look wonderful in black leather.

Not good, Juliet sternly reminded herself. Keep your mind off his body and on his protocol.

"Yes, well..." She fidgeted with the array of forks to the side of the china plate, part of a set that had been a gift from the Royal Family of Holland. "Do you know what this is?"

"A fork," he replied helpfully.

"What kind of fork?"

"A silver one?"

"What kind of silver fork?"

"A royal silver fork?"

"It's a fish fork. You can tell by the different tines."

She went on to list each of the eight pieces of flatware. And then quizzed him on each one.

"These people have way too much time on their hands if they're so obsessed with which fork to eat with and when," Luc declared in exasperation after he'd misidentified the first-course fork as the salad fork.

"Do you want to return to conversation 101?" she warned him.

He waved his hand in surrender. "No, no, let's stick with flatware, by all means. I'm simply fascinated by flatware. Tell me more," he invited with a mocking gleam in his devilish eyes.

So he thought this was funny did he? She'd teach him a thing or two. "The first fork was used in the eleventh-century but it took eight hundred years before it was universally used in western cultures." She went on until his eyes glazed over. "Are you getting bored, your majesty?" When he didn't answer, she repeated, "Your majesty?"

"Huh?" he said with a startled oh-you-mean-me look.

"I asked you if you were bored by my lessons?"

"You're a very good teacher. It's just that there's only so much one can comprehend about the tines of a fork before it all becomes hazy in one's mind."

"A king can't afford to allow his mind to become hazy, your majesty."

"I told you to stop calling me that."

"And I told you that you need to get used to hearing it, and to responding to it."

"You know, I think I'm starting to love it when you use that prissy voice on me."

She stood up, straightened her shoulders and said, "That's not an appropriate comment."

"You wanted me to respond, right? Well, I'm respond-

ing. Come on, Juliet. Loosen up.'' The next thing she
knew Luc had taken hold of her hand and tumbled her
onto his lap.

Grinning down at her with devilish sexiness, he started
tickling her just beneath her right ribs, where he knew
she was particularly vulnerable. But Juliet squirmed just
as he reached for her, and his hand brushed her breast
instead of her ribcage.

They both froze.

Chapter Four

Juliet's startled gaze flew to his. She was so close she could almost drown in the rich blue of his eyes. Perched as she was on his lap she was all too aware of the intimate differences between male and female. She could feel the magnetism flowing between their bodies.

She couldn't move, couldn't breathe, and certainly couldn't look away. He appeared as caught up in the moment as she was. Her parted lips were mere inches from his. She could feel his warm breath on her mouth. Was he leaning closer?

Desire and anticipation were like a fire dancing over her sensitized skin.

Then she was set back on her feet as suddenly as he'd tugged her onto his lap.

What had just happened? Had he been about to kiss her or had she imagined that?

Luc's smile was sheepish. She knew hers was awkward. The air between them seemed to hum. Each of them hurriedly moved away—retreating to a separate area of the dining room as if afraid of what might happen otherwise.

Juliet tried to read Luc's emotions from his expression, but his years at Interpol had given him the ability to hide his feelings when he wanted them hid. The only thing she caught was him staring at her as if trying to read her mind. Could he guess that she'd wanted him to kiss her? Was he regretting joking around with her? Was he sorry he'd tumbled her onto his lap? Should she say something? Make a joke? Try and break the ice? Or make a run for it in an attempt to save face?

That last option sounded darn good to her at this point.

"I think we've done about all we can for one evening," she said briskly. "We'll arrange the next tumble...I mean tutorial in the stables."

Tumble in the stables. She tried not to blush at her verbal slipup. Had he noticed?

"That sounds fine," Luc said, his voice as smooth as ever. "I suppose no one would get suspicious if we were to bump into one another there."

"Nothing suspicious at all," she quickly agreed. "You bumped into me earlier."

"Right," he agreed just as quickly. "I bumped into you and there was nothing to it."

"Absolutely nothing," she said with cheerful brightness. "One friend bumping into another."

"With a little horseplay thrown in on the side. The stables would be a good place for that," he said. "For horseplay, I mean."

Smooth, real smooth, Dumont, Luc told himself. *This is Juliet you're talking to here. Why this sudden attack of nerves? You weren't this jumpy when you had your first weapons training exam.*

But then, caressing her breast had been as explosive as handling live ammunition.

He honestly hadn't been trying to cop a feel when he'd pulled her onto his lap. It hadn't been a premeditated move on his part at all. She'd just been acting all starchy and distant and he'd simply wanted to tease her into remembering that they were friends.

Instead he'd raised an entirely new issue. And that wasn't all he'd raised.

His reaction to her feminine body had not been a platonic one. He wanted to kiss her, and he almost had before he'd come to his senses. He might not have the protocol manual memorized yet, but he was pretty darn sure that seducing Juliet would *not* be deemed appropriate behavior.

Seducing Juliet. Where had that idea come from? Probably from the raging arousal that still held his body in its taut grip. But where had this entire reaction come from? He'd known Juliet for years and had never even placed her and seduction in the same sentence before.

Maybe he'd been too long without a woman. That must be it. He'd been searching for the missing heir for months and that had left him with no time for anything else, including romantic relationships. And the year before that he'd dated several women, but hadn't found one that really held his interest.

His job and the long hours he kept had proved to be a stumbling block as far as long-term relationships with a woman went. And now there was this king thing.

"So I'll meet you in the stables tomorrow," Juliet was saying. "Will three in the afternoon be convenient?"

"Sure," he replied although he had the sudden feeling that nothing about this entire situation was going to prove the least bit convenient at all.

* * *

Juliet was in love. She had no doubts whatsoever about that. And what's more, her love was returned tenfold, perhaps even a hundredfold, by the objects of her devotion—two-month-old kittens from the stable cat, Rexxie.

The purring balls of fluff were stretched out on her lap with utter faith in her ability to keep them safe. How wonderful it must be to have that kind of trust. She hadn't felt that way since her father had died. Her mother had loved him so intensely that she'd never quite recovered from his passing.

One of the kittens wiggled and tucked his head under his brother's leg to get more comfortable. Juliet had named the gray-and-white one Mittens and the black-and-white one Rascal. She wasn't allowed to have a pet while she lived in the palace and having one at boarding school certainly hadn't been allowed. While attending her first semester at the Sorbonne in Paris she'd shared a cat named Mignon with her older roommate Cleo, who had taken the cat home with her to Provence upon graduation.

Paris was a beautiful city, but Juliet had become homesick, so she'd transferred to the local university here in St. Michel where she'd completed her degree and graduated with top honors. She was now working on her advanced degree in history.

This morning she'd been in her office supposedly working on reading the diaries and private letters of Queen Regina, but instead had spent much of her time daydreaming about Luc and reliving that moment last night when he'd tumbled her onto his lap.

Why had he done that? He'd just been kidding around, one friend to another, she told herself as she'd done a hundred times over the past fifteen hours. He didn't mean anything by it.

And that moment when their lips had almost touched? When his hand had touched her breast? The kitten stretched and snuggled its silky head against the very same breast Luc had touched. She could still feel the warmth of his hand, as if it had been imprinted through her skin to her very heart.

Looking down, she blushed at the sight of her nipples showing through her white shirt. She'd removed her formal riding jacket so she wouldn't get fur on it while playing with the kittens.

Her appearance in the stables hadn't aroused any suspicions, because she'd been a frequent visitor since the kittens had been born. The stablehands didn't even notice her, which was fine by her. Juliet had never been the kind of female a man noticed.

She'd never minded that before. She was smart and that had always been enough for her in the past. And then Armand Killey had come into her life, with his charming ways, sweeping her off her feet.

But Armand had just been using her. After she'd confronted him about his deception, he'd at first tried to deny it before realizing the game was up. Furious at having his plan backfire, Armand had said some scathing things to Juliet—telling her no one would love her for herself, that she lacked the elegance and class of a true royal, that she was the gangly, ugly stepsister.

He'd hit her where she was the most vulnerable.

Juliet had no royal blood in her veins. The king had only been her stepfather. And she wasn't elegant or gorgeous like her stepsisters, the royal princesses, or adorable and charming like her half sister, twelve-year-old Jacqueline.

She'd thought at the time three years ago that she'd been broken-hearted. Then Luc had come into the palace and into her life. And the longer they knew one another, the more she suspected that while Armand had severely damaged her self-esteem as a woman, he'd never truly touched her heart. Luc, on the other hand, seemed to have the key to her heart. And that made her entirely too vulnerable.

Whereas Armand had hurt her deeply, Luc had the power to destroy her. Not that he ever would intentionally. But the very fact that he was the heir to the throne of St. Michel meant that there were some pretty insurmountable differences between them now.

While Mittens slept on her breast, Rascal woke up and started playing with his own tail, tumbling over backward as he did so. In an effort to save him from falling off her lap, she stuck her legs straight out so he'd roll down her thighs to her knees. The kitten scrambled back up her trousers to the safety of her lap. Luc wasn't as lucky. He tripped over her shiny riding boots and landed face-first in a pile of hay.

Great way to make an impression on a king, she thought to herself as she quickly set the kittens back into their basket and hurried to Luc's side.

"I'm so sorry. Are you okay?"

He got up and plucked the hay from his dark hair, while shooting her a wry glance. "If you wanted to take a tumble in the stable with me, all you had to do was ask."

"It was an accident," she protested. "I had two of the kittens on my lap and one was about to fall off, so I…"

"Tripped me?"

"I put my legs out and you stumbled over them. You should have watched where you were going."

"Me? You're the one who created a hazard."

"They didn't teach you how to avoid falling over

someone's feet in all your Interpol training?" she automatically teased him as she had many times in the past before remembering who he was now.

As if able to read her thoughts, he cast her a warning glance meant to remind her that they were not alone. Leaning close, he whispered in her ear, "Don't you dare your highness or your majesty me here."

His breath was warm against her skin and smelled of coffee. She wondered if she'd taste coffee on his lips. Unable to resist touching him, she pulled a few bits of hay from his hair. "You look like the scarecrow from the *Wizard of Oz*." If the Wizard had been played by a young sexy Pierce Brosnan perhaps.

"Was the scarecrow the one who lacked a heart?"

"The scarecrow lacked courage, which you have tons of. The Tinman was the one who lacked a heart, which you also have."

"Not everyone would agree."

"You've definitely got a heart," she whispered, sliding her hand down to his chest. "I can feel it beating."

Again their eyes met and time stood still. As had happened last night, Juliet was swept up in a wave of sensual awareness. Her surroundings melted into the background, and all her attention was focused on this one instant in time, on this one man in the universe.

She felt the throb of his heart beneath her palm, felt the warmth of his skin through the cotton of his riding shirt. Her own heartbeat was pounding so loudly she was surprised Luc couldn't hear it.

"Luc, I didn't see you there." The interruption came abruptly and caught them all by surprise. The stablehand named Pierre appeared disconcerted to have walked in on them. "Is there something you need?"

What Luc needed was his head examined for allowing

himself to think of Juliet this way. What had come over him? By this morning he'd convinced himself that last night had been a momentary lapse, a freak occurrence never to be repeated.

Yet here it was, just a few hours later and again Juliet was getting to him. His life was complicated enough at the moment, he certainly didn't need a romantic entanglement to further muddle things.

"No, Pierre, I'm fine," he belatedly replied, stepping away from Juliet and, he hoped, from further temptation. "I just thought I'd take one of the horses out for a ride."

"Monarch is feeling frisky today, why don't you take him?"

Luc knew all about feeling frisky. "I'll do that, thanks for the suggestion."

"I've got Annabelle saddled and ready for you, ma'am," Pierre added with a shy smile for Juliet.

"I already told you to call me Juliet," she gently scolded him, her smile brightening her entire face. "Thank you, Pierre."

"Not at all, ma'am, I mean Juliet."

"We'll both be there shortly," she added.

Pierre nodded and reluctantly walked away.

"That young man has a giant crush on you," Luc told her.

"Don't be ridiculous." She scooped up the basket of kittens.

"I'm not being ridiculous, I'm being observant. Didn't you see the way he blushed and tripped over his own tongue when he spoke to you?"

"Pierre is just shy."

Luc reached out to gently rub one of the kitten's ears. It was Mittens, who adored ear-rubbing more than anything except for the cooked chicken Juliet sneaked in from the royal kitchen.

Seeing Luc's slender but large hands on the tiny kitten made her melt inside. His gentleness made her think he'd be good with a baby. It was the first time she'd thought of him and children. She wanted children herself. Only the other day she'd realized that her mother had been married and pregnant by the time she was Juliet's age.

"What are you thinking about?" he asked her.

She could hardly say "your children" so she replied, "Our next lesson."

"We've barely started this one yet," he noted.

"I suspect you'll do fine on a horse." He certainly looked fine in the formal riding attire. The crisp white shirt was none the worse for his tumble in the hay, and the dark jacket and tight-fitting jodhpurs hugged his body like a glove. She quickly looked away before he could practice his eye magic on her, drawing her into his gaze. "Ballroom dancing is next."

He grimaced.

There wasn't time to say anything else until they'd both mounted their horses and begun their ride. Even then, Luc waited until they'd cantered some distance from the palace in the royal park, well beyond the formal gardens, before pulling Monarch to a halt and turning to face her.

"Ballroom dancing?" he repeated.

"Don't tell me you don't know how to dance."

"The last dancing I did was at a Sting concert, and somehow I doubt that the movements will be the same in this case."

"Not unless you were doing a waltz at the concert."

"Waltzing was frowned upon," Luc noted dryly.

"Well, it's not frowned upon at a formal ball. I'll meet

you in the Crystal Ballroom just before midnight tonight.''

''Are you planning on wearing your covert operations outfit again?'' he inquired.

''Now you're planning my wardrobe?''

Luc shrugged. ''It's just that if you're going to teach me how to dance in a formal situation like a ball, then perhaps you should dress appropriately.''

''If someone sees me walking down the corridor in a formal ballgown they're bound to get suspicious,'' she pointed out.

''Then let's compromise. Wear that black slinky dress you had on the other week for the ballet gala.''

She frowned. ''Slinky? I don't have anything slinky. Oh, you mean that black slip dress? It *is* a favorite of mine. I got it at a vintage clothing store in Paris.''

''Wear that and I'll be a happy man,'' Luc stated.

He might be a happy man, but she'd be a very vulnerable woman, moving closer to falling even more in love with him with every second.

Juliet looked at the clock for the tenth time in as many minutes. She even went over to the mantelpiece to make sure it was working correctly. After all, the timepiece was almost a hundred years old and had been stashed in the palace attic for most of that time. The glass was missing from the face, but the elegantly painted cherubs dancing around the outer edge were exquisite.

Everything in the two rooms assigned to her—a large sitting room/bedroom and an attached drafty bathroom—had either been rescued from the palace's attic or basement.

Junk, Celeste had proclaimed in disdain, preferring her own royal apartments with their ivory chaises and gilded cabinets. But Juliet loved the comfy feel of her surroundings, where nothing was perfect, but everything blended together in a way that made her smile.

Blue was her favorite color, and that showed, from the faded blue damask of an armchair to the delicate robin's-egg blue in a series of watercolors of Venice. Sure the chair had a few lumps; she just sat around them. And yes, the watercolors had age speckles along the edge, but that just endeared them to her all the more.

As in her office, a large Oriental rug covered the floor and books covered almost every available space. A few smaller items on display, like the porcelain figurine of a mother and child, had been purchased by her at some out-of-the-way shop in Paris or St. Michel catering to those who liked unique pieces.

Indeed, her college friend had referred to Juliet's decorating style as "Paris Flea Market" and told her it was all the rage now.

Juliet studied her reflection in the slightly cracked rococo mirror. The black dress Luc had ordered her to wear did go well with her pale coloring and dark hair. But there was no way it was slinky. Was there?

She turned sideways and sucked her tummy in. She even attempted to take a few regal steps before wobbling on her high heels.

Juliet never had mastered the art of walking in these darn things. She was tempted to wear flats, but Luc was right in his assessment that for the lesson to be most beneficial they'd have to recreate the actual atmosphere of a ball as best they could in the circumstances. He was even bringing music. She wondered if he planned on bringing a Sting CD.

She smiled and tried walking again. Better this time.

Not regal by a long shot, but no longer as dorky or book-ish.

Of course, the logical, practical side of her brain was sternly warning her that it shouldn't matter how she looked, what she wore, or how she walked because she was merely tutoring Luc. It wasn't as if they had a date or anything.

Guard your heart, she warned her mirror image, who showed no sign of heeding her words if the grin on her face was any indication. You'd think she'd just been given a huge box of dark chocolates or something, the way her face was beaming.

Her smile faded as she remembered the baby gift that she'd sent to Celeste's apartment that afternoon. It had been returned by the footman Henri, one of the few servants Juliet couldn't warm up to, along with a note from Celeste.

I hardly think a toy giraffe is appropriate for the new king of St. Michel, since giraffes are not regal animals. It is my hope that you were not trying to insult baby Philippe II with your paltry present.

Most of the time, Juliet simply tried to keep out of Celeste's way. After her mother's death, it hadn't taken King Philippe long to find a replacement. Celeste was a beautiful woman, with classy features and lovely blond hair. But the class was only skin deep—and it had nothing to do with the fact that, like Juliet, she lacked any royal blood. No, her commonness had more to do with her behavior than her background.

Not that Celeste couldn't be sweet and charming when the occasion warranted it. She could. And that surface brightness blinded some to her true nature. But not Juliet.

Enough thinking about Celeste. It was almost midnight, the magical witching hour. She had to hurry or she'd be late.

The Crystal Ballroom was located on the main floor toward the back of the palace, facing the gardens. The huge rectangular room got its name from the series of priceless Austrian crystal chandeliers on display—three large examples placed down the center of the long room and three smaller ones at each shorter end of the room. The elaborate design created a tiered waterfall of crystal drops, each one mirroring a rainbow of colors as they reflected the light. The first time Juliet had seen them, she'd felt as if she were standing in the middle of a rainbow.

The famous chandeliers weren't illuminated tonight. Instead Luc had set a series of candles on the sideboard.

It wasn't the first time she'd seen him in a tuxedo, but her breath always caught at how devastatingly handsome he was in the formal attire. The impeccable cut emphasized the athletic fitness of the strong body beneath—the broad shoulders, the lean torso, the narrow waist.

His mouth was quirked into a teasing smile as he murmured, "Well, do I pass inspection?"

"You'll do," she replied a tad breathlessly. "I see you brought the music." She nodded toward the portable stereo system on the Italian marble floor. "Is it Sting?"

"No, it's Strauss. I borrowed some CDs from the prime minister. He has an amazingly vast and diverse collection, everything from Mozart to Duke Ellington to the Beatles."

"Strauss is good for waltzing."

"So is that dress," Luc noted approvingly. "I'm glad you took my suggestion and wore it tonight."

"Suggestion?" she repeated with a lift of one brow. "An order was more like it."

"Does that mean I'm sounding more kingly already?"

"I told you from the very beginning that you were already a pro at giving orders."

"Yes you did, and I appreciated the vote of confidence."

"That's what friends are for," Juliet replied with deliberate cheerfulness. The look he'd just given her when he'd commented on her dress a moment ago was still making her heart hum. Nerves were clearly fueling her imagination, because she could almost have sworn that a smoldering sexual interest had been present in the depths of his gorgeous eyes.

Hah, that'll be the day, she thought to herself. Luc looking at her as anything other than a buddy.

What about the other night? that nagging voice in her brain demanded. *What about the almost kiss? Or that moment in the stables when his eyes met yours...?*

Get real, she ordered her fanciful thoughts. You can't afford to get caught up in this fairy-tale moment. Don't do it. Don't play the fool the way you did with Armand.

"All right then," Juliet said crisply, as she did whenever she started a lesson with Luc. "Let's get started. I'd like this lesson to be more productive than the one on dining. We never did get around to things like olives."

"Olives?" Luc lifted one elegant eyebrow at her in a gesture she recognized and was coming to love.

"Yes, olives. One must always take olives with a spoon and never a fork. Here, I've written up a list for you." She handed him a neatly folded piece of paper.

"I suppose I mustn't drink my soup, either, hmmm?" he teased her.

She flushed. "You asked me to help you."

CATHIE LINZ 63

"So I did and I truly appreciate the help. I'll look over your notes later when I'm in bed."

She could picture him in bed—his bare chest with a tantalizing whirl of dark hair leading down to his navel, the white sheets gathered down around his narrow hips, barely covering him.

Suddenly the ballroom was unbearably hot. She would have fanned herself with a sheet of paper, but she'd just handed it over to Luc and she wasn't about to grab it back again. She'd just have to pretend nothing was happening, that her hormones weren't going into overdrive.

"Yes, well…" She cleared her throat and began again. "As I mentioned earlier in the stables, I believe you'll find the waltz the most useful dance. We'll start with the basic position, your hand curved around my waist, your other hand clasped in mine."

"What about white gloves?" Luc suddenly said. "I'm not going to have to dance in white gloves am I?"

The mental image of him dancing in white gloves and nothing else had her stumbling over her own two feet.

"Steady there," he murmured, catching her in his arms.

"I'm not that good a dancer," she said, embarrassed by her inability to focus. "You'd do better with someone else."

"I don't want anyone else," he said.

If only that were true. If only he really did want her as something other than a friend.

"And don't even think about turning me over to the protocol minister," he warned her. "Can you see me dancing with him?"

Juliet had to smile. "No. If you don't like the protocol minister, there's always the Privy Council."

"Not one of whom is a day under seventy."

"I'm sure the prime minister is."

"Yes, but any group that makes the prime minister look like a spring chicken isn't a group I want to dance with. *Capiche?*"

Her smile had turned into a full-blown grin by now. "*Capiche.* Your fluency with so many languages will serve you well as..."

Luc placed his finger over her lips as he had the other night. "The walls have ears," he warned her.

She firmly moved his hand away from her mouth. She was not about to succumb to temptation tonight. She was going to be practical from the get-go. "I still don't see why you have to be so secretive about this news."

"Remember what happened with Sebastian? The tabloids were all speculating that he was the heir and the announcement was almost made that he was. I don't want something like that happening again. Which is one of the reasons I wanted independent confirmation of everything I learned in France about my true heritage."

"And what's the other reason?"

"The Rhineland situation needs to be addressed plus I wanted some time to learn the royal ropes, so to speak."

"Speaking of which, we should resume our dancing lessons. We don't have all night."

"Why not? Do you have someplace else you have to be?" he demanded.

"Yes," Juliet teased him. "I've got a hot date waiting to pick me up outside the palace walls."

"You'd better not," Luc growled, surprising her with the intensity of his voice.

"Why not?"

"Because of this..." Without further ado, Luc kissed her.

Chapter Five

Juliet didn't know who was more shocked—herself or Luc. She did know that being kissed by him was better than she'd ever imagined, and she'd imagined it very often in vividly sensual detail.

But none of those fantasies had prepared her for the sheer pleasure of the real thing. The candlelight flickered against the walls, showing their shadows merged together. She closed her eyes and focused on his mouth, returning his kiss with fervor.

His lips were warm and unexpectedly soft. They were also seductively hungry and erotically intent.

Tilting his head in the opposite direction, he targeted her mouth again, his lips parting hers in a sensual dalliance that made her knees melt.

He slid his arms around her, his hands burning through the thin silk of her dress as he clasped his fingers at the base of her spine and tugged her closer. She felt the smooth material of his tuxedo jacket beneath her fingertips, smelled the burning candles.

She felt as if she, like those candles, was going up in flames. She had known with a feminine instinct that he was destructive to a woman's reason, but she had no idea how powerful a distraction he could be—wiping out all thought of propriety or common sense and replacing it with sheer sensation.

Flickers of desire soared upward from the depths of her body. She felt the thud of his heart against her breast and knew her own nipples were rubbing against the fine material of his jacket. She should be outraged, she should be embarrassed, but she was neither. He made her shiver and burn at the same time with a powerful response that she couldn't control.

His mouth promised an ecstasy beyond belief, while his tongue tempted hers to come play an erotic game of hide-and-seek. Her lips parted even farther. He quickly accepted her invitation, his tongue darting inside to explore the dark recesses of her mouth even as his hands explored the curve of her derriere.

She was intoxicated with pleasure, gasping for breath as he shifted his kisses along her face to nibble at her ear.

The moment's respite was all it took for reality to reassert itself.

"What are you doing?" she whispered, whether to herself or him she couldn't be sure.

"Kissing you," Luc whispered in reply, his voice as hazy as hers.

"You shouldn't."

"Why not?"

"Because you're…*you* and I'm…"

"You're Juliet," he murmured against her lips. "You smell like lemons and taste like heaven."

"Do you say that to all your friends?"

Friends. The word doused Luc like a bowl filled with ice water. He had no business kissing her this way. He immediately released her and stepped away.

"Sorry," he said curtly, turning away so she wouldn't see the effect she'd had on his body. "I don't know what came over me."

Liar, he silently mocked himself. He knew damn well. Ever since he'd tumbled Juliet onto his lap the other night, he'd known she was getting to him. He wasn't sure why. Why now? Was it fate's way of laughing at him? Of turning every single corner of his life upside down, including his friendship with Juliet, a friendship he'd come to rely on strongly. The idea of ruining that friendship was one of the few things that truly scared him.

But this newfound sexual awareness of Juliet as a woman was also more than a tad disconcerting. She was ten years younger than he, and much more inexperienced. He had to be the responsible one here. He should have been the one to come to his senses first, instead of her questioning his motives.

She'd been right to call a halt to things when she had, before they had gotten completely out of hand. In the middle of a ballroom, for heaven's sake.

It had to be the candlelight and the music. He marched over to the portable stereo and leaned down to hit the Stop button with so much force the electronic equipment skidded on the marble floor.

There, that should be better. He turned to face Juliet. "Again, I'm sorry about that."

Juliet was at a loss for words. What could she say? That she wasn't the least bit sorry? That she'd loved every minute of it? That would be an understatement.

"You were just trying to be a friend by helping me out here," he continued, "and I took advantage of that."

A friend. That dreaded word again. Juliet wished she could obliterate it from their vocabulary. But if she did that, what was she left with?

"Do you want to continue the lesson or would you rather call it quits for tonight?" he asked her.

"What do you want?" she asked in return.

Luc looked at her for a moment, his sensually brooding gaze seeming to indicate that he wanted *her*, before he turned away from her.

"I want my life back," he said, his voice harsh. "I just want my damn life back."

"I demand to speak to the Privy Council!" Celeste angrily informed the prime minister first thing the following morning.

"No one is allowed to speak to the Privy Council, aside from the king and he is no longer with us."

"My *son* is the king," Celeste declared.

"The Privy Council would have to make that determination," the prime minister calmly replied.

"Which is why I must speak to them. It's been nearly a week since my son Philippe II was born, yet still they refuse to make the proclamation declaring him king."

"And you know the reason why. You are aware of the fact that King Philippe was married to Katie Graham and that together they produced a child—possibly the heir to the throne."

"I know that the dowager queen has been telling such stories, but that is all they are. Stories. Figments of her imagination."

"It is more than imagination. We have documentation."

"I can supply experts who will say that your documentation is a forgery," Celeste countered, narrowing her eyes. "There is already talk that you and the dowager queen concocted this story to keep my child from the throne. Is the Privy Council aware of this fact?"

"I will inform the Privy Council of your concerns."

"Of course you will," she mocked him.

"If you doubt my word about speaking before the Privy Council, you have only to read the Royal Charter of St. Michel. It is all there. In the case of questionable succession, the Privy Council will meet and discuss the situation. No member of the royal family is allowed in on those discussions. The Privy Council includes the prime minister and four noblemen whose families have held the position for hundreds of years."

"I also know that it states in the Royal Charter that if there is no male heir then St. Michel reverts back to Rhineland."

"That is not going to happen," the prime minister firmly declared.

"And it's not going to happen because *my* son is the male heir, the only son of King Philippe."

"The Privy Council is waiting for me. I must go, ma'am."

"Oh, you'll be going all right," Celeste muttered as she watched him walk away. "Right out the palace door, the minute I'm in charge of things. I don't need you or your musty old Privy Council. I've got more powerful allies than you'll ever know."

Juliet spent the entire morning immersed in the early 1800s. It was better than dealing with her own life in the present day.

Luc's kisses last night had left her tossing and turning all night. No matter how she tried, she couldn't get the memory out of her mind. The texture of his lips, the taste of his mouth, the tantalizing swipe of his tongue against the roof of her mouth. All these things and more took control of her senses, put her in danger of *losing* her senses.

She'd come to work early, determined to make some major headway in her research reading. She'd fallen behind schedule because of Luc.

She had completed one section of Queen Regina's diaries and was ready to move on to the next volume when something outside caught her attention. The sun was shining as it often did this time of year in St. Michel, and the flowers in the garden basked in the light. The irises were past their peak glory but still put on a colorful display—from pale yellow to darkest purple. But it was the woman who'd just entered the garden who made Juliet pause. She appeared distressed as she hurried across the path toward the gardener's quarters at the back of the palace. It was Yvette, the head gardener's wife.

Perhaps she was just in a hurry to return home. Juliet knew that Yvette had recently had a baby, and she had meant to give her a baby gift. She had one wrapped in her quarters all ready to go, but all her spare time was spent preparing lessons for Luc—or lusting after Luc. The bottom line was that Luc had distracted her.

She was also distracted by the sight of something shiny out of the corner of her eye. Turning, she saw that it was a large foil box of candy and it was being held by Luc. Actually, he was waving it as if it were a white flag of surrender.

"I come bearing gifts." Luc took a few steps into the room, as if to gauge her reaction before deciding to proceed further. Apparently deciding it was safe, he came in and elegantly propped himself on the corner of her desk. He waved the now-open box practically under her nose. "Chocolate, to apologize for my behavior last night. I was in a strange mood and had no right venting my frustrations on you.''

His words stopped her in midreach for a dark chocolate truffle. ''Is that what kissing me meant to you? Venting a few frustrations?''

''No, I meant afterward. When I said I wanted my life back and called off the lesson.''

''And went storming off, don't forget that part.''

He didn't hesitate. ''And went storming off.'' He paused as if unsure what to say next.

He looked so awkward that Juliet had to say something to break the ice. ''So you kissed me to avoid dance lessons, is that it?''

He smiled. ''Yes, that's it.''

They both knew it wasn't, but there was a certain shared relief in falling back on old familiar friendship patterns. She took a chocolate. ''You're a devious man.''

''A devious man with chocolate.''

''Which makes you all the more dangerous.'' She popped the truffle into her mouth before closing her eyes in ecstasy.

''And hard to resist?'' he asked hopefully.

''Impossible to resist,'' she said. ''How did you know these are my favorites?''

''I know a lot of things about you.''

''Like what?''

''Like the fact that you lose pencils at an alarming rate, that you have a weakness for vintage clothing and kittens. And a talent for looking beneath the surface dents to see the real beauty beneath.''

She wondered if that was a talent he had, to look beneath her bookworm appearance to the real her.

''Other people see junk,'' Luc said. ''You see... possibilities.''

She had the feeling that they were no longer talking about furniture here. "Because I see the possibilities in you?"

He nodded.

"I'm not the only one, Luc. The dowager queen and the prime minister both admire you so much."

"The Privy Council is meeting again today."

She nodded. "I know. I still have that letter from your mother, if you're ready to read it."

"I'm not," he said curtly.

She knew he would be, someday. And when he was, she wanted to be by his side.

The Privy Council wasn't known for moving quickly. Glaciers were speedier than this noble body of elders. Today's meeting had lasted the entire day and well into the evening. It was days like this that made retirement look very pleasant to Prime Minister René Davoine.

While the prime minister had gone to his office to check on the day's business, the Privy Council had taken an early and extended dinner break before returning to the Privy Council Meeting Room for after-dinner cognacs and cigars.

Opening the ornately carved heavy wooden door, René had to wave his hand in front of his face to clear some of the cigar smoke from the room. It was so thick he couldn't even see the series of dour portraits hanging from the dark paneling along the walls. Peering through the stale air he could just make out the other four members of this elite group. All wore heavy red velvet robes and matching white wigs dating back to the eighteenth century.

Prior to the present situation, St. Michel hadn't had a meeting of the Privy Council since 1866, when it had been alleged that the oldest son had been borne to the king's mistress and that the rightful heir was the second son. The Privy Council had met then to look over the documents and make a decision. It had taken them four years.

Today's members showed a similar inclination to be snail-like in the speed of their decision-making. They had first come together after King Philippe's death and had hit several bumps in the road since then. This was not a crowd for bumpy roads.

Baron Severin was the oldest and therefore the self-proclaimed leader. White-haired and a bit hard of hearing, he had the upright bearing of a military man. By contrast, the Duc de Montreaux was noticeably bow-legged, caused by his lifelong enthusiasm for riding. Sir André DeVallis and Count Baptiste Rivaux looked very much alike. Both men were balding with florid faces and very rotund builds. Neither did much talking.

"Gentlemen," René said. "I'm here to see if you have reached a decision about Luc Dumont's claim to the throne."

"*Eh?*" Baron Severin bellowed, having refused to wear his hearing aid because it interfered with the fit of his wig. "Luc's on the phone?"

"His claim to the throne," René corrected, speaking succinctly and as close to the older man's ear as he could. "Has the Privy Council reached a decision?"

"These things take time, my boy."

Baron Severin was the only one who would think that at age sixty René was a boy.

"I fear that Queen Celeste may be about to make trouble," René warned them.

"That confounded woman has been trouble since the moment King Philippe got engaged to her," the Duc de Montreaux proclaimed.

"It's a shame the days when the Privy Council had to approve a royal engagement are over," Baron Severin said.

The other three solemnly nodded their agreement.

René tried to get them back on track. "Be that as it may, gentlemen, may I remind you that you still need to make a decision regarding Luc Dumont."

"Fine fellow," Baron Severin said.

"Excellent head of security," Duc de Montreaux agreed. "I say we keep him on."

René sighed, gathering his tattered patience before reminding them, "We have the birth certificate stating that he is the son of King Philippe and Katherine, also known as Katie Graham."

"Well, now, it wouldn't be the first birth certificate we've seen proclaiming someone to be their son, now would it?" Baron Severin in turn reminded him. "We're still awaiting confirmation from the authorities in France that the documentation is indeed true and accurate. You cannot hurry these things along, my boy."

"St. Michel needs its king, gentlemen. We have been without a monarch long enough," René said.

"You really think this Luc is the one?" Count Rivaux asked, speaking for the first time.

"I do," René replied.

"And you believe he will carry the de Bergeron family name with dignity and honor?" Baron Severin asked.

René nodded. "I do. Luc is a serious man. He isn't one to take duty lightly. I do not believe there is a frivolous bone in his body, in fact."

"Is that so?" Duc de Montreaux said from beside the window. "In that case, what is he doing slipping out the back of the palace with that young filly Juliet in tow?"

Chapter Six

"**W**here are you taking me?" Juliet demanded breathlessly as Luc hurried her down a garden path, away from the palace.

"To a carnival," he replied. "We've been working hard, it's time we took a break."

Luc was casually dressed in black jeans and a black T-shirt. He was the epitome of a sexy cat burglar, moving with an elegant smoothness and speed. Pulled along behind him as she was, she had the most tempting view of his body, his slim waist tapering to lean hips and long legs. And his derriere…even thinking of it as a royal posterior didn't slow down her racing heart.

She had to say something to break the sexual tension building within her. She focused on his dark clothing.

"Are we going on some kind of covert mission?" she inquired with what she thought was an admirably good example of friendly cheerfulness.

"Let's just say I'd rather not announce my presence to the paparazzi."

"They've been hounding the palace ever since that rat Wilhelm sold the story about King Philippe's marriage to Katie to that tabloid."

"I know." Luc led her to the edge of the formal gardens. "That's why I tightened security around the perimeters of the grounds."

She paused, cautiously eyeing the thick forest before them. "If you're planning on walking through the woods to avoid detection, I have to warn you that I'm not dressed for it." She waved a hand down at her vintage 1950s black sundress. "You should have told me to wear slacks."

"There's no need for that." Luc wasn't about to admit that he liked looking at her legs. "We're not going through the woods." He paused before a huge oak tree on the edge of the woods, walking around it to pull out…a gleaming motorcycle.

Juliet eyed it distrustfully. "I'm not dressed properly to ride on the back of that thing."

"Yes, you are," he assured her. "Come on, hop on. We're not going far. You can tuck your dress around your legs."

"Easy for you to say," she muttered.

"Do you want me to help?"

"No, you stay where you are," she ordered him, resting her hand on his shoulder as she daintily mounted the motorcycle.

Luc felt her wiggling against him as she arranged the skirt of her dress. Her breasts brushed against his back, and her legs bracketed his.

A familiar fire smoldered within him. It wasn't the kind of flame that flared to life the instant he saw her; it was the kind that grew in intensity each time they were together. Instant lust he could deal with, but this overwhelmingly powerful attraction was something else entirely.

"I should have worn black leather," he heard her mutter, and almost groaned aloud at the sexy fantasy of her dressed like a biker babe—her thighs barely covered by a short skirt, her breasts pushing against a tight T-shirt. His body responded to the hot images, forcing him to shift position, which only made her thighs rub against his even more.

When had his sweet innocent friend Juliet turned into a sultry sex kitten?

"I'm ready," she informed him.

He was ready, too, so ready that his body was about to explode. A flick of his wrist and the well-tuned engine roared to life.

"Hang on tight," he told her and she obeyed, plastering herself to him.

The night air was deliciously cool against his flushed skin as he drove down the path leading past the stables to a little-used service road. He nodded at the guards on duty before stepping on the throttle and letting the Harley have its way.

Juliet pressed her face against his back and closed her eyes, not in fear but in pleasure. Now she could concentrate on the enjoyment of being so close to him. She could smell the fresh scent of his soap, could feel the warmth of his skin through the cotton of his T-shirt. She had her arms wrapped around his flat stomach, her hands gripping his sides. She could feel him breathing.

Her lips automatically pursed in a tiny kiss before she realized what she was doing. Turning her face so that only her cheek rested against his back, she opened her eyes and tried to focus on the passing scenery but it was going by too quickly.

"We're almost there," Luc yelled over his shoulder, as if sensing her sudden restlessness.

He might have sensed it, but he couldn't know the reason for it. Reality had reared its ugly head once again in her mind. A king on a Harley. The days when Luc would be able to take off like this were limited. She knew that would be very hard for a man like him, a man who valued his independence and freedom.

She would be there for him, she vowed. To help him adjust.

And then what? The taunting question demanded an answer. Then do you sit by like a good little girl while he marries some gorgeous princess?

Oh, do be quiet, she silently ordered her wayward thoughts. Let me just enjoy this evening for what it is, a night out with Luc.

Luc stopped the Harley on the carnival grounds a few minutes later. The colorful lights of the various rides reflected off the metal of the motorcycle as he dismounted with ease and turned to help her. Her skirt had somehow hiked up during the ride, and was now at the mid-thigh mark. Before she could rectify that matter, Luc put his hands on her waist and lifted her from the back of the bike as if she weighed no more than a feather.

When she'd given him the first lesson in the royal dining room, and he'd talked to her about biking to classes at Cambridge, she'd fantasized about him riding a gleaming motorbike. And here he was. Her fantasy come to life, grabbing her by the hand and hurrying her along to the carnival's entrance. There might be flashing clown faces instead of cherubs, but to Juliet this was heaven, sheer heaven.

A large arch lit their way, flashing lights perched on top in a garishly cheerful illumination. This was no classy night at the ballet, Luc silently noted. He hoped Juliet wouldn't be disappointed.

The place was crowded, mostly with young people. Teenage girls in shorts, tank tops and body glitter roamed in packs, pausing to giggle and whisper whenever they saw a group of their male counterparts. Teenagers in St. Michel were the same as teenagers in the rest of the world. Out to have a good time.

Luc could relate to that. He had the same goal tonight. To have a good time and not think about the future.

The midway was lined with rides that tilted, rolled or shook. But it was the Ferris wheel that caught his eye. "Let's go on that first."

"I'm not very fond of heights," Juliet warned him.

"Just hang on to me," he replied.

That she could do, having perfected "hanging on" while sitting behind him on that motorcycle. As she boarded the Ferris wheel with Luc at her side, Juliet wondered how many more fantasies of hers would be fulfilled tonight.

The ride started gently enough. It was only as they were lifted higher and higher, that a flutter of anxiety hit her.

"Don't look down," Luc advised, taking her chin in his hand and gently lifting her face skyward. "Look up. Look at all those stars."

It was a glorious spring night. The dark sky was dotted with sparkling pinpricks of light, a divine necklace strung together across the heavens. And there, just above the horizon, a golden full moon was rising. It truly was a magnificent sight.

"It's magical," she breathed.

"Magical," he agreed, looking at her instead of the sky.

The ride ended too soon, and Juliet insisted on taking another before Luc laughingly demanded they move on to the next one.

An hour later they stopped at the food tent for a meal of sausage and crisp *pommes frites*—french fries—which they washed down with chilled red merlot from one of the many local vineyards. St. Michel was well-known for its wines. For dessert they had freshly made cotton candy wrapped around paper cones.

As they left the eating area, Luc happened to see a father with his small son. The man held the boy's hand, and the child looked up at his father with awe and delight.

The scene reminded Luc of when he was that age. Had he ever looked up at Albert that way? Was that why he felt this stupid ache in his chest?

Or was it because the man he had believed to be his father all these years wasn't his father after all?

Not that Luc had spent a lot of time with Albert. Once Luc had reached the age of eight, school had become his home—first Eton then Cambridge. While at university, Luc had become good friends with Jeremy Landing, the son of a high official in Interpol. Luc had spent several summer vacations with Jeremy and his family. He'd preferred doing that to dealing with the tension between Albert and his second wife, feeling like an outsider in what was supposed to be his own home.

Jeremy's father, Spencer, had been impressed with Luc, who spoke five languages fluently and had excellent grades in all his subjects at Cambridge. Spencer had been the one who'd suggested that after leaving university, Luc should consider a career in Interpol.

It seemed like a great idea to Luc. Interpol, an international police force, was an appropriate home for someone who felt that he belonged nowhere in particular.

Luc still felt that way, as if he belonged nowhere in particular. This despite the fact that he now had blood relatives—a grandmother, several half sisters, a baby half brother.

But he couldn't seem to get comfortable with the idea that he was no longer on his own. And he couldn't seem to get comfortable with the idea of his future being locked into the strict codes and traditions of royalty.

This was where blind passion had landed them all. In a carnival house of mirrors—where nothing was as it seemed. His mother and King Philippe hadn't been able to be practical and control their emotions, so they'd run off and married. And now look at the convoluted mess they'd left behind.

Luc gave the father and son a brooding look, angry at the tug he felt at his heart, the tug of a little boy who'd had a father and then lost him to a second marriage. He'd rightly told Juliet that he avoided love because it left you feeling too vulnerable. Not giving a damn was a much saner, a much more sensible way.

His gaze shifted to Juliet. He didn't seem to be able to be sensible about her. Yet sometimes it felt as if she was the only sensible and solid thing left in his life. During this past week she'd been his Rock of Gibraltar. When it had felt as if everything else in his life had been turned upside down, Luc had only to look at her and feel better.

The trouble was that looking at her didn't merely make him feel better. It also made him want her. So, in a way, even his relationship with Juliet had changed. Because in the past few years, while he'd always considered her to be a good friend, he'd never gotten sexual ideas about her. But all that had changed.

Now he thought about her when he restlessly tossed in

his bed at night. He dreamt about her, about that kiss they'd shared in the Crystal Ballroom the other night.

Luc felt as if he were a man on the run from his own destiny, a destiny not of his own choosing. So here he was tonight, playing hookey like a kid who'd run off to join the circus.

"Everything all right?" Juliet asked him.

"Yes. Come on, let's try our luck at one of the booths."

"Win a tiara for the lady!" a burly bald man invited with the feigned cheer of a natural-born salesman. "Come on then, sir, win a bright and shiny bauble for your pretty sweetheart."

"What do you say?" Luc turned to ask Juliet. "Wouldn't you like a tiara of your own?"

"Doesn't every girl long for a tiara of her own?"

She'd just been kidding, but Luc took her seriously. "Here." He handed over some money to the vendor who quickly counted it.

"This will give you ten chances to hit the red center of the target with one of these balls," the vendor said.

"I won't need that many," Luc confidently replied.

In the end he was right. He hit the target on his fifth try. The vendor grudgingly handed over the prize before turning his attention to more customers.

Luc led Juliet to a small stand of trees that afforded them a bit of privacy before turning to her and bowing. "Your tiara, m'lady." He placed it on her head before standing back to admire his handiwork. "It looks good on you."

She laughed and shook her head, making the tiara slip to one side. "I find that hard to believe."

"Why is that?"

"I'm not the royal type."

"Neither am I," he noted quietly.

"Luc, I'm sorry." She placed a hand on his bare arm. His skin was warm beneath her fingers. "I didn't mean to bring that up. I know you're trying to forget it all tonight."

"That's not as easy to do as I thought."

"I'm sorry," she repeated, reaching up to remove the tiara.

"No." His hand stopped her. "It does look good on you. You look good."

She laughed self-consciously. "I'm sure I have mustard on my chin and there are probably remnants of cotton candy on my cheek."

Luc cupped his hand beneath her chin and lifted her face. Leaning down to study her closely, he declared, "No mustard. Not a trace. The cotton candy claim may need further investigating, however."

He completed that investigation with his lips, tasting his way from her left cheek across her lips to her other cheek and back again. "Mmm," he murmured against her mouth. "Sweet, very sweet."

It *was* sweet—and hot and tempting. And when he leaned away to grin at her, Juliet wished they weren't just pretending, wished they really were just a man and a woman out for an evening of fun. Instead she worried about him getting into trouble for being out with her.

He's the king. Who's going to yell at him?

Yes, Luc would be in charge, but he would also be expected to behave in a certain way and required to conform to rigid standards. Kissing her at a carnival did not conform. She was not suitable. She was no European aristocrat, she had no royal blood of her own. She was just a commoner who was falling in love with a king.

Not a wise move, to be sure.

"Come on," Luc said as he had all evening, once again grabbing her by the hand. "There are still a few sights we haven't seen yet."

He headed them toward the other side of the midway, pausing in front of a fortune teller's tent. "Let's see if she says there's a crown in my future," Luc said with that contagious smile of his.

The interior of the tent was so dark Juliet had to pause to get her bearings. In the center was a woman seated at a table, with a bright light shining down on a crystal ball and a deck of tarot cards. The fortune teller had a brilliantly patterned scarf wrapped turban-style around her head. Large gold hoop earrings hung from her ears and a pair of gold front teeth flashed in her mouth as she gave them a huge smile. "Welcome, come in, sit. Let me tell you about things to come. I am Magda and I do it all—read palms, tea leaves, tarot cards, the crystal ball. Which would you prefer?"

"Which one has the highest degree of accuracy?" Luc asked as he held out one of the chairs for Juliet before taking the other for himself.

"Ah, for you, I think reading the palm would be best." Magda quickly reached for his hand and turned it over to study it closely. "Hmmm, very interesting. You have a split life line here. Which means that you will be leading two lives, each one very different from the other. And your love line is interesting, too. I see conflict and confusion here. Your health line is good but has several fractures, times when you have been in great jeopardy. I see a time like that approaching you. Wealth is coming to you soon as well, a great deal of wealth. But it is uncertain whether it will bring you happiness."

Luc snatched his hand away. "Do my friend's hand now."

Juliet tried to ignore her irritation his calling her a friend had caused. Magda took Juliet's hand and said nothing for the longest time. "You are very smart, and you see more than most. You have one great passion in your life. He is tall, dark—"

"—and handsome," Luc supplied.

"And in danger," Magda corrected him. "The outcome is still unsure at this point." Looking Juliet in the eye, Magda added, "But I sense that you are an old soul and are prepared to fight for your future. I wish you luck, miss, and I fear you will need it."

After paying Magda and going back outside, Luc said, "Well that went as expected."

"You expected her to tell you that you're in danger?"

"I expected that tall, dark and handsome would come up. I hoped in your reading and not in mine," he added with a roguish grin.

But Juliet couldn't smile. The fortune teller's words had unsettled her. "She said you were in danger, doesn't that bother you?"

"Not really. It wouldn't be the first time I was in danger. Listen, all that hot air made me thirsty. Let's go get a drink."

And he was off again, this time leading her to a small concession stand that had been set up to one side. The striped red-and-white colors made it easy to spot, and it was the only place to get a drink on this side of the midway.

Luc sat Juliet at a nearby bench while he stood in line. When he finally placed his order, they were all out of everything except for the local beer. The vendor indicated a barrel filled with ice and told him to pick out his bottles.

Luc did so, turning his back to the metal pole holding up the tent canopy.

A moment later the heavy metal pole crashed down on him.

Chapter Seven

"Luc!" Juliet cried, leaping to her feet and running over to the fallen concession tent.

The collapsed canopy covered everything now, preventing her from seeing him.

"I'm okay," Luc's voice was muffled by the heavy canvas.

The vendor came scurrying around from the back, apparently not caught up in the collapse. "I am so sorry, so sorry," he kept repeating as he enlisted the help of some passing men to lift the remnants of the heavy canopy and free Luc.

When she finally saw Luc emerge, she almost cried with relief.

"Are you sure you're okay?" she demanded, running her hands down his arms as if needing to verify for herself that he hadn't broken anything.

"I'm fine. It would take more than a stupid canopy falling on me to hurt me."

"Luc, that heavy metal supporting pole narrowly

missed you and believe me that was capable of doing plenty of harm had it connected with your head or your back.''

"But it didn't. It was just one of those stupid accidents, like almost getting hit by a piece of falling masonry from the palace the other day.''

His words made her go cold in the gentle warmth of the night. "Whaa...at?" Her voice sounded as shaken as she felt.

"You know where they've recently set up that scaffolding along the edge of the south wing to do some repair work? Well, I was walking by when half a gargoyle or something fell down, narrowly missing me. The thing must have weighed a ton. It shattered on the pavement.''

"Why didn't you say anything?" she demanded, infuriated by his nonchalant attitude about his own safety.

"I gave the construction foreman a fiery lecture about on-the-job safety.''

"I mean to *me*. Why didn't you say anything to me?''

He raised one dark brow, indicating his surprise at her vehemence. "Because it wasn't important.''

"Of course it's important. There's a pattern here. Twice in the past few days you've almost been seriously injured.''

"Oh, please.'' He rolled his gorgeous rich blue eyes at her. "This incident tonight is nothing. A gust of wind probably knocked the canopy down.''

She wasn't buying that for one minute. "There isn't a spit of wind tonight, it's completely still.''

"There's no way someone would have known I would be standing beneath that particular canopy on this particular night.''

She hated it when Luc used that logical tone of voice on her. "They would if you were being followed."

"You really do have a vivid imagination."

She hated it even more when he didn't take her seriously. "Stop acting so nonchalantly about all this. I'm worried about you."

"I can see that. It's the first time in decades that anyone has worried about me. But there's no need."

The thought of no one worried about him for years and years made her heart ache. His mother had died, his stepmother was worse than useless, and his father had apparently forgotten about him once he'd shipped him off to boarding school.

At least Juliet had her older brother Georges to depend on, and her younger sister Jacqueline. But Luc had grown up with no one—no one to fuss over him, no one to worry about his well-being, no one to love him.

Her thoughts were interrupted by the agitated voice of the vendor offering them free beer, before he realized that the fallen canopy had knocked over the barrel filled with beer bottles and smashed them all.

"That could have been you," Juliet said, pointing to the smashed debris that the men had just uncovered.

"But it wasn't. I can't live my life with could-have-beens. Especially not now."

She wasn't about to let him off the hook. "Now is when you have to be especially careful, Luc. There are people who will not be pleased with your...discoveries about your past. People who have a lot to lose. And there are still some dissident Rhinelanders who want St. Michel annexed to their country so they can have river access. Who knows what they might have planned? You can't be cavalier about your safety, Luc. I couldn't bear it if anything happened to you."

"Nothing is going to happen to me," he promised her. "Nothing at all."

"Did you do it?" Celeste whispered to her lover Claude Guignard as she welcomed him into the private apartment she'd rented in St. Michel. No one at the palace knew about this place, located near the river, where she let her sensual side have free reign—red velvet couches and chairs in the living room, a leopard-print bedcover and mirrored ceiling in the bedroom. This pied-à-terre was where she plotted her future. "Have you killed him yet?"

"It's not that easy to make it look like an accident."

She pulled away from him to bestow an icy look of disapproval. "Which means no, you haven't killed him."

Claude cringed as if dreading what she might do or say next. "The falling masonry should have worked. I followed him tonight to the carnival and successfully collapsed a tent on him."

"A tent?" she repeated, mocking him. "A lethal weapon to be sure."

"There was a heavy metal pole that almost made a direct hit, but he turned at the last minute."

Her cold expression was warmed by a sudden smile and a thoughtful expression as she drifted into the living room. "There may be a better way. Killing him was perhaps a tad too obvious. We may still be forced to do that, of course. But I'm exploring other options."

"Other options?"

"Yes. I've arranged for a top secret meeting here and have invited a very important guest."

"Who is it?"

There was a discreet knock on the door. "Ah, that

should be him now. You'd better open it, the queen shouldn't be seen doing something so menial.''

Claude did her bidding, as he always did.

Celeste had her most gracious smile in place as she greeted her visitor. "I'm so glad you could make it here this evening."

"Your invitation was too intriguing to refuse, Your Majesty," Berg Dekker replied, taking her hand and bowing over it before kissing it with just enough flirtatiousness to make Claude's brown eyes flash with jealousy.

Berg was a tall man with ice-cold features. He'd earned the nickname Iceberg because he so coldly went after what he wanted in business, regardless of who or what got in his way. The environmental fanatics claimed his petroleum and chemical plants were major polluters. Celeste really didn't care. The important thing was Berg's enormous wealth and influence. He gave buckets of money to his pet charities, cultural foundations and political causes. His power joined with hers would make a formidable alliance.

"Claude, you know Berg Dekker, one of Europe's most powerful and successful businessmen. And, as you know, Berg, Claude is St. Michel's deputy energy minister."

"If this is about that money that changed hands several months ago..." Claude began nervously.

"Do be quiet, Claude," Celeste chastised him. "This meeting isn't about the bribes you've been taking from Berg for years."

"It isn't?" Claude almost sagged with relief.

"No, of course not. I admire you and Berg for making an arrangement that was beneficial to you both. Claude, do get our guest some wine."

He did as she ordered.

"A toast." Celeste raised her crystal wineglass. "To a mutually prosperous future."

When Berg touched his glass to hers, she saw the interest in his pale blue eyes. She sank onto the couch, striking an elegant pose in her designer outfit—a chic Valentino cocktail dress that showed off her great legs. "Do sit down." She patted the couch on either side of her. Berg chose to sit at her right, Claude got the seat that was left over. "The matter I wish to discuss is much larger than a few bribes here and there. Berg, I know how passionately you have supported the cause of Rhineland annexing St. Michel. And I know that while you have patriotic reasons for your views, you also have practical reasons. You are in the lucrative petrochemical business—refining and transportation. This business would be made easier and less expensive if you were to have access to the St. Michel River, leading to and from the North Sea, correct?"

"Correct."

"Then I have what I hope will be an irresistible proposal for you."

"Everything about you is irresistible," Berg murmured in a charming voice.

"You are being too kind." Celeste fluttered her eyelashes at him before crossing her legs, showing a generous amount of thigh. "I fear I'm not looking my best after having given birth to the heir to the throne a mere week ago."

"You are looking ravishing with that special glow that only a new mother could display." Berg lifted her hand to his lips. "The best paintings by Raphael and Rembrandt pale in comparison to your beauty. And I should know, as I have rather an extensive collection of artwork, one that would put the royal collection of St. Michel to shame.''

''It is a shame that St. Michel was taken from Rhineland,'' Celeste murmured.

''That is my view,'' Berg agreed. ''For hundreds of years we ruled this area. Then some rabble-rousers demanded independence and forcibly took our rightful heritage from us.''

''That was way back in the sixteenth century,'' Claude pointed out in an affronted voice. ''And some would say that the group Rhinelanders for Annexation are a bunch of rabble-rousers,'' he added, clearly unhappy about the fact that Berg still held Celeste's hand.

''Of course, anyone who said that would be wrong,'' Celeste stated with a warning look at Claude. ''My proposition is one that would benefit us all. I've learned that you have quietly been supplying a great deal of the funding for Rhinelanders for Annexation, Berg.''

''There is no law against that.''

''Of course not. But I think you and I can work together to get what we both want.''

''Why would you want to make a deal with us?'' Berg asked. ''You have a son, a healthy baby boy. There is no threat of St. Michel returning to Rhineland due to a lack of a male heir.''

''Actually the problem we have is that we have too many male heirs,'' Celeste said. ''I trust that this meeting and everything that is said here will be held in the utmost confidentiality?''

Berg nodded. ''You have my word.''

''Mine, too,'' Claude hurriedly added.

''Good.'' Her smile reflected her pleasure. ''It would not be in any of our best interests for word of this conversation to get out.''

"What did you mean by saying there are too many male heirs?" Berg asked.

Celeste leaned closer. "You have no doubt heard the ridiculous story about King Philippe's youthful marriage to that American girl named Katie Graham."

Once again, Berg nodded. "Yes. And I know that Luc Dumont has been searching for the child they are rumored to have had together."

Celeste appeared surprised. "I wasn't aware that that was public information."

"It isn't, but I do have my sources."

"The story, of course, is a total fabrication." She waved her hand dismissively. "A way for Prime Minister Davoine to hang on to power. He knows that the moment my son becomes king, I will fire him for being an incompetent fool, and replace him with someone like Claude here. Someone loyal to me."

"I'm assuming then, that Luc found someone he believes to be the heir?" Berg noted astutely.

"Yes, but that's not important. As I said, the entire story is a fabrication. However some people may be fooled by these lies. So I need a way of uniting the people of St. Michel. If I were to present the country with a solution to the vexing Rhineland problem, then naturally they would all support me in their gratitude."

Berg's pale blue eyes narrowed suspiciously. "What kind of solution?"

"I propose that we share the rights to the river. That way you would save millions in shipping costs, since you would no longer have to pay the local taxes and tariff. We would also be more lenient in our regulations on the cargo sizes of your barges and the number of barges you can use at any one time. I understand the current regime has been making life difficult for you, shutting down your operations because of pollution concerns despite Claude's best efforts to look the other way. That would not be a problem if we were to enter into a partnership—a silent, secret partnership.''

Berg's expression went from suspicious to calculating. ''What exactly is it you want from me?''

''I want your support, as leader of Rhinelanders for Annexation, for my plan.''

''I am not the leader,'' Berg protested. ''I am merely one of many patriotic souls who feel our country has been wronged.''

Celeste smiled. ''Come now, there's no need for any false modesty here. You are the power behind the organization. Those men they arrested a few weeks back were merely the figureheads. *You* possess the real power.''

Berg's icy eyes showed a flash of admiration. ''Not many have figured that out.''

''Like you, I have my sources.'' She shifted against him, subtly brushing her body against hers. ''So what do you say? Do we have a deal?''

Berg smiled. ''Yes, Your Majesty, it appears that we do.''

''Shhhh,'' Juliet cautioned Luc with a giggle. ''You're going to wake everyone up.''

''I'm not the one making noise, you are. How many of those free beers did you have?'' The vendor had insisted on treating them, sending his son to get another case of beer to make up for the unfortunate incident involving the tent canopy.

''None. I'm drunk on life.'' Juliet smiled as she dreamily danced her way down the garden path leading to the palace, which looked romantic in the moonlight with its golden sandstone walls and towers creating a fairy-tale silhouette against the night sky. Most of the many windows were darkened at this time of night. But the Cheval de Roi fountain was illuminated, its trio of rearing horses seeming to hover above the water. "Wait."

"What for?"

"I want to make a wish." She dug into her purse. "Did you know this fountain is rumored to have magical properties?"

"I think after that fortune teller at the carnival, we've had enough magic for one night."

"No, this is different. I've been reading the diaries of Queen Regina and she writes about it there. The horse in the middle represents King Philippe's great-grandfather's prized stallion. And the two females flanking him were thought to represent his wife and his mistress."

"The stallion's?" was Luc's mocking reply.

"No, the king's. And once the fountain was up, no horse from the royal stables ever lost a race. The fountain became known as a lucky place, a place to make dreams come true. You can't look at the horses when you make your wish, you have to turn away from them in deference."

"Fascinating, I'm sure."

"It is. Which is why I'm going to make a wish." She removed a coin from her purse and, turning her back to the fountain, quickly tossed it over her left shoulder where it fell into the fountain's water with a distinct plop. "Here, I'll give you a coin to make a wish, too."

"I don't make wishes—" Luc began when Juliet interrupted him.

"Oh no!" she wailed.

"What's wrong?"

"The coin! That was my special lucky coin. One my

mother gave me that I carry with me all the time. I didn't mean to use that. I need it back."

"You can't get it back."

"Yes, I can. I'm going after it. You stand guard and make sure no one from security comes by."

"I *am* security."

"Then close your eyes. I'm going in." She kicked off her shoes and carefully waded into the fountain. "My goodness, that stallion is certainly well-endowed," she noted as she bent beneath it to get to the center of the fountain.

"Stop eyeing the equestrian private parts and get your fanny back here," Luc ordered her.

"Not until I get my lucky coin." She plodded through the water, raising her skirt even higher to avoid getting it wet.

"Oh, for heaven's sake," he muttered in exasperation. "It's dark out here. You can't see what you're doing."

"I can, too. The fountain is lit. Oh, I think I see it!" She leaned forward eagerly, a tad too eagerly as it turned out, because an instant later she lost her balance and fell onto her derriere.

"I didn't realize you'd be doing a water ballet to-night." Luc's voice was filled with laughter. "Or is it synchronized swimming you're performing? If so, I'm going to have to mark you down for a lack of finesse in your landing."

"I'll give you a lack of finesse." Juliet reached out to swipe her hand along the water, creating a giant splash that doused Luc and left him blinking at her in surprise.

Noting the dangerous gleam in his eyes, she quickly started scooting away. "Now, Luc, you started it by in-sulting my lack of finesse. What are you doing?" She eyed him suspiciously. "Why are you taking off your shoes?"

"Because I don't want to ruin them when I come in there after you."

"You don't have to come in. I've got my coin." She held it aloft and stood up, her cotton dress clinging to her like a second skin. "I'm coming out. As soon as you take a few steps away from the fountain. Not *into* the fountain." He showed no signs of obeying her. "Luc, be sensible."

"I am being sensible. As head of security I found a strange and unauthorized object in the fountain. It's up to me to remove it."

Juliet placed her wet hands on her equally wet hips. "Luc Dumont, you get out of this fountain this instant!"

"Now, Juliet, you know how that prim voice of yours drives me wild."

"I mean it, Luc." She backed up until she was up against one of the equine statues' flanks and could go no farther.

"I'm sure you do."

"It was your own fault you got wet. You taunted me. And you know how I hate being taunted."

"Yes, I know. I also know that you're rather fond of this." He wrapped his arm around her waist and tugged her to him. Leaning down, he brushed his lips across hers.

"Mmm, that is rather nice," she murmured against his mouth.

"Nice?" He drew his head back to give her a reproachful look that melted her knees. "Only nice? Clearly I'll have to try harder."

Wrapping both arms around her, he lifted her against him as he devoured her mouth with a hotly sensual kiss that had her parting her lips and greeting his tongue with her own. The splashing sound of the fountain's water mimicked the beating of her heart in her chest. The wet material of her dress provided little protection as her thighs were pressed against his, making her very aware of his arousal.

She felt her nipples tingle and firm. He dabbled the wet point of his tongue along the roof of her mouth as his right hand shifted to cup the soft swell of her breast.

Looking down on them from a window on the second floor, Baron Severin tsk-tsked disapprovingly and told the prime minister, "René, I fear this Juliet girl may not be a good influence on our future king. I think it's time the dowager queen had a talk with those two."

Luc found the summons waiting for him when he arrived at his office just after sunrise. He hadn't gotten much sleep after kissing Juliet in the fountain last night. He got hot just thinking about it. He couldn't believe he'd made out with her like some randy teenager.

The sound of one of the palace guards beginning his nightly rounds had finally brought him to his senses last night. He'd helped Juliet scramble out of the fountain, then watched her as she grabbed her shoes and ran barefoot into the palace without saying a word to him.

And now he found a message on his desk announcing that the dowager queen wanted to see him the moment he came in. Knowing she was an early riser, and knowing she liked having her breakfast served in the sunny Emerald Salon just outside her rooms, he figured he might as well get this over with.

"Ah, Luc, how nice to see you." She smiled and gestured to the chair beside her. "Come, join me for breakfast."

"Some coffee would be nice. Black, please," he requested of the footman.

The dowager queen allowed him two sips before starting her inquisition. "I hear that you and Juliet were cavorting in the fountain last night."

It was all he could do not to spew his coffee all over the priceless tablecloth.

The dowager queen patted him on the back with surprising strength. "There now, we can't have you choking. Not after all this work went into finding you." Turning to the footman, she dismissed him before returning her attention to Luc.

"Your highness..." he began.

She interrupted him. "You may call me Grandmother. Some of the girls call me Grandmama on occasion, which I find endearing, but I thought Grandmother would be more comfortable for you."

Luc couldn't think of one comfortable thing about this entire situation.

"Baron Severin from the Privy Council was a little...chagrined, shall we say, when he saw you two last night. The man doesn't have a romantic bone in his entire body."

"What was he doing spying on me?"

"Actually he was just looking out of the palace window. He had no idea the wild scene he'd be witnessing."

"You make it sound as though we were indulging in some kind of orgy or something," Luc protested.

"Were you?"

"Of course not! Juliet isn't that kind of woman."

"What kind is she?"

"You've known her longer than I have."

"In years, perhaps. But Juliet has always kept her distance from me. I have the impression of a bookish young woman who is more comfortable reading about the past than living in the present.''

"She was living in the present last night,'' Luc said.

"Apparently so.'' The dowager queen's blue eyes sparkled as she pinned him with one of her piercing stares. "I'll make you a bargain. If you promise to call me Grandmother, and to have tea with me every day this week, then I'll assure the prime minister and Baron Severin that there's nothing to worry about, that you and Juliet were merely having fun in the way young people today do.''

He set down his coffee cup with a distinct clink. "That's blackmail.''

"How else am I to get to know my grandson better?''

"You could try asking. A strange concept for a monarch maybe,'' Luc noted in irritation. "But an effective one nonetheless.''

"Asking? Hmmm.'' She sipped her tea before gracefully returning the delicate china cup to its matching saucer. "An interesting concept, to be sure. All right then, Luc. Will you have tea with me this week?''

"No,'' he said without hesitation. "Not *every* day. But I will spend some time with you. Providing you don't try to interrogate me about my private life again.''

She bestowed a regal stare upon him. "My dear boy, had I wanted to interrogate you, you'd know it, believe me.''

"I'm fairly good at interrogations myself,'' Luc warned her, not the least bit intimidated.

Her smile widened. "I do believe I'm going to enjoy having you as my grandson, Luc.''

Chapter Eight

Juliet noticed the furtive looks Yvette, the head gardener's wife, was giving her before the morning's weekly staff meeting began. She prayed it wasn't because Yvette had seen her with Luc in the fountain last night.

Oh, but it had been divine. Standing in the moonlight, held in Luc's arms and kissed the way a man kisses a woman he wants. But was it the way a man kissed a woman he *loved?*

She knew she loved him. She'd suspected it for ages, had been inching closer with every breath she took. But last night, when Juliet had returned to her rooms, she'd known. She loved him.

The thought of Luc being hurt by one of the accidents that had befallen him lately was enough to make her sick at heart. And angry. Furious, in fact. No one was going to hurt the man she loved. She'd do whatever it took to protect him.

Which is why she was speaking at the staff meeting this morning. Everyone—from the lowest of housemaids to the valets and footmen to the palace steward and the royal chef himself—gathered in the staff dining room just off the kitchens.

The air was still filled with the warm aroma of the cinnamon buns that had been freshly baked that morning, and a small vase of freshly cut roses adorned the spotless table. Alistair, the palace steward, had previously worked at Buckingham Palace and he prided himself on the small finishing touches.

"Thank you all for allowing me to speak to you during your meeting," Juliet said. She knew almost all of them by name.

"As you are aware, things have been very stressful since the king's death. I don't have to tell you all how volatile the situation could easily become. There are some in Rhineland who avidly support annexing St. Michel. Now, our security is in excellent hands with Luc Dumont. He looks after the safety of us all. I just thought that during these difficult times, we could repay the favor by helping him out a bit."

"How can we do that, miss?" Andrea, one of the housemaids, asked.

"By keeping our eyes and ears open, by reporting anything suspicious to Luc, no matter how inconsequential you might think it is."

"We like Luc," the chef declared on everyone's behalf. "He doesn't put on airs like some people."

"He gave a big contribution when my daughter needed that surgery last year," one of the footmen said.

"And he gave my son a stern lecture when he was getting into trouble," another said. "Turned him right around, our Luc did. My son is doing just fine now, getting good grades."

"Of course we'll help out Luc, in any way we can," Alistair promised. "You can count on us."

The stories and their support warmed Juliet's heart. She had no idea Luc had quietly been helping those in need. Luc, of course, had never said a word. He wasn't the type to go blowing his own horn, to brag about his accomplishments or his generosity. He was a doer, not a talker.

Which boded well for the people of St. Michel. They would soon have a wonderful new king. But their gain would be Juliet's loss.

Although, if she were honest with herself, she'd have to admit that there was a tiny part of her that had started to secretly hope once again. It wasn't logical and it wasn't practical but... Those looks he'd been giving her, and more important those kisses they'd shared. Their relationship was at a new crossroads. The problem was that each path ahead held its own dangers.

Luc could do worse than to marry her. The rebellious thought chased its way across her brain. Certainly no one would love him more than she did—no one could.

But Luc wasn't looking for love. He'd said as much himself. Which meant he'd be looking for someone compatible with his new lifestyle. And while Juliet certainly knew her way around the palace, it wasn't the same as having a royal bloodline. There was simply no substitute for that. Plus there was the matter of hating to be in the spotlight, another strike against her in the royalty department.

"Juliet, the dowager queen asked me to give you this." One of the footmen held out an envelope on a silver tray for her.

She took it with some trepidation. Why would the dowager queen be writing her? She opened the wax seal and removed the fine parchment paper. "Your presence is required for tea this afternoon. I've decided it's time you interviewed me for your paper on the history of St. Michel's royal women."

Generally speaking, Juliet tried to avoid the dowager queen as she tried to avoid Queen Celeste, albeit for entirely different reasons. Queen Celeste had never appreciated Juliet's presence in the palace. After all, Juliet was the child of her husband's former wife. But since Juliet was no threat, either in her beauty or her need for attention, Celeste usually ignored Juliet.

The dowager queen, on the other hand, had a way of intimidating not just Juliet but almost everyone she came in contact with. Lately, Celeste had been promoting rumors that the dowager queen had gone "dotty" in her old age. Juliet wasn't buying it.

The dowager queen possessed the type of regal presence that was hard to find these days. It dated back to Queen Victoria's time, when monarchs were monarchs and no one questioned their authority. In Victoria's case, this meant that she forbade new servants to look her in the face. Instead they had to keep their eyes firmly on the floor at her feet.

Juliet would have been glad for such a ruling in the de Bergeron Palace, because the dowager queen had the most piercing blue eyes she'd ever seen. They weren't rich and filled with depth like Luc's. They had a way of taking you apart inch by inch and finding all your faults.

Not that the older woman had ever voiced any criticisms. She didn't have to. One look from her said it all. Which left Juliet wondering what the dowager queen would be saying to her this afternoon.

Teatime arrived all too soon. Juliet had tried to bolster her sagging confidence by wearing a lovely dress with a

Liberty print of tiny flowers. The dress was made for a tea party. Well, not really. She'd gotten it in a little shop during a visit to London. But it did have the look of a tea party somehow. At least in her mind. And, she hoped, in the dowager queen's as well.

She'd restrained her hair into a French braid with help from one of the maids and had taken special care with her makeup, which had to be discreet but not non-existent.

She'd brought a notebook and pen with her, to take notes. The dowager queen had promised to tell her story, and Juliet was hoping she could add the information to her own research.

The dowager queen's apartments were in the south wing, on the sunny second floor overlooking the fountain and the gardens at the back of the palace. The rooms all possessed a stately elegance and none more than the White Drawing Room where they were having tea.

Juliet paused for a moment to simply appreciate her surroundings. Straight ahead were ceiling-to-floor French doors, which opened onto a terrace. In front of them stood graceful marble statues and tall lapis lazuli vases overflowing with irises. In one corner of the room was a French Florentine cabinet inlaid with panels of semi-precious stones. And in the other corner was the dowager queen.

"Ah, there you are, child. Well, don't just stand there. Do come in."

Juliet performed a brief curtsy as her mother had shown her when they'd first moved to the palace.

The dowager queen beamed at her in approval. "Your mother taught you well. No one knows how to curtsy properly these days. It's not taught at school any longer, and it should be. Where would the world be without civility and manners, I ask you? In my day, things were very different. Why, when I married King Antoine, the women all curtsied when I walked down the aisle. And the event certainly wasn't filmed the way they are these days. That bad trait started with Princess Grace allowing her wedding to be filmed.'' Her expression turned disapproving.

Juliet was a longtime admirer of the beautiful actress who had become a princess. ''I've read that she only did that in order to dissolve the remaining seven years on her movie contract with MGM.''

''Perhaps, but those Grimaldis have always been a wild bunch. The de Bergeron family is much more traditional. My father was a grand duke, so I was raised in the ranks of St. Michel's aristocracy and taught the rules of protocol and propriety from birth.'' She paused a moment to give Juliet a thoughtful look even as she indicated with a royal wave of her hand that Juliet should be seated beside her. ''Perhaps it's wrong of me to have you curtsy. After all, I am almost family.''

That one word, *almost,* created a huge gulf. One that, for the first time in her life, Juliet was glad of. Otherwise, she would have been related to Luc, and that would have been more than she could have borne.

''Jacqueline is my granddaughter and you are her half sister. Do you take sugar or milk in your tea?''

''Milk, no sugar, thank you, ma'am.''

The dowager queen handed Juliet a cup of tea in a delicate china rimmed with roses. Quickly setting her notebook and pen on her lap, Juliet took the teacup and prayed she wouldn't spill anything.

The dowager queen tilted her head regally, her short dark hair meticulously in place, her powder-blue suit just

a shade darker than her piercing eyes. "Jacqueline is due
back from Switzerland soon, isn't she?"

"Next week."

"She's a handful, that girl is."

"As are many of the de Bergeron women," Juliet felt
compelled to point out. She might only be Jacqueline's
half sister, but she loved her dearly and wasn't about to
let anyone speak badly of her.

With a nod of her head, the dowager queen indicated
that the footman on duty was to offer Juliet a selection
of tea sandwiches and goodies from a three-tiered serving
dish.

Juliet paused to admire the swan-shaped dainty bit of
frosted sponge cake as well as a huge strawberry dipped
in white and dark chocolate to resemble a tuxedo.

"Take one of the strawberries, they're delightful this
time of year." The order was implicit even if the older
woman's tone was aristocratically charming.

Juliet did as she was told.

"So you're writing a paper on the de Bergeron
women." A new level of interest had entered the dowager queen's voice.

Juliet set her plate on a side table. She couldn't eat
and speak at the same time, not with someone as overwhelming as the dowager queen. During all their previous meetings, other family members had always been
present, mitigating the impact the older woman had.

"Yes, ma'am. Actually I'm doing a thesis on the role
of women in St. Michel's royal history. I've just been
reading the journals of Queen Regina who, as you know,
lived in Queen Victoria's time. She had eight children
and, like Victoria, she saw them all well married to the
heads of other royal houses across Europe. When her
husband the king had a stroke, she took on his duties

herself and ran the country quite successfully. She was a wise and compassionate queen."

"The power behind the throne, eh? No doubt that's what Celeste was hoping for."

"I wouldn't exactly describe her as either wise or compassionate." The words were out of Juliet's mouth before she could stop them.

The dowager queen cackled with laughter. "Well said. So you're not as quiet and sweet as one might think. Good. I like a person who speaks her mind."

"Then, if I may be so bold, might I ask why you invited me here for tea today?"

"I called you here today because I wanted to get to know you better. I understand you've been spending a great deal of time with Luc."

"Luc and I have been friends for a long time."

"That's all? Just friends?"

"Yes." Juliet prayed that lightning wouldn't strike her for telling a bold-faced lie to the dowager queen.

"Hmm." The older woman subjected her to one of her piercing stares, her light-blue eyes slicing right through her. "As you know, Luc's station in life will soon be changing dramatically."

"I'm aware of that, ma'am."

"I know. Luc said that he'd told you about it even before coming to the prime minister and me."

"He only did that because—"

She waved Juliet's words away with an imperious wave of her elegant hand. "You don't have to defend him to me, child. Although it's admirable that you'd want to. It's not my intention to interrogate you about your private relationship with Luc. As his grandmother I'm merely trying to learn more about him."

"Then you should really speak to him."

"I've tried to." The dowager queen leaned forward in agitation, her thin hands resting on her gold-filigree topped cane. "The impudent young pup says he doesn't have time for tea with me."

"I'm sure he meant no disrespect, ma'am."

"Oh, he came nicely enough yesterday morning and sat on the very chair you are in now, looking all elegant and handsome. He does have the most divine eyes, doesn't he?"

Juliet had to smile. "Yes, ma'am. He does."

"And the most stubborn nature. How do you deal with him?"

"By letting him be himself," Juliet replied, "and accepting him for who he is."

"I'm well aware of who he is. Although he insists no one else know until that confounded paperwork comes through from the French authorities. It should come any moment now. The two independent investigators that Luc also insisted we hire have told us they'll have their final report within the next forty-eight hours with Luc's DNA results."

"So soon?" Juliet's stomach clenched at the thought of how little time they had left.

"St. Michel has been without a king long enough. Celeste has been agitating to have her infant son named as the heir. The impudence of the woman! When there have been rumors for months about her having an affair, even before my poor son passed on. Who knows if her child is really my son's? She refuses any DNA testing for the infant. That woman will never rule St. Michel, not as long as there's breath left in my body!"

The flush on the older woman's cheeks concerned Juliet, as did her labored breathing. "It can't be good for you to get so upset, ma'am. Would you like me to call someone?'' The footman who had served them earlier had departed.

"No, no, I'm fine." The dowager queen patted Juliet's hand. "There's no need for concern. I'm not about to…how do those Americans put it? Ah, yes, I'm not about to kick the bucket just yet."

"I certainly hope not, ma'am."

"I intend to stick around for some time yet. After all, I've got a new grandson and I want to see him crowned as our next king. And I want to see him married and have children of his own to aggravate him."

"Luc would be an excellent father," Juliet murmured, remembering how gentle he'd been with the kittens out in the stable.

"I heard he took you to the carnival. Don't look so surprised, very little occurs in this palace that I'm not aware of."

"He just needed a bit of time away from all this."

"It pains me that he is having trouble accepting the changes in his life."

"He needs time. His entire life has been turned upside down," Juliet gently reminded her.

"I understand that. What I don't understand is why he won't speak to me about it."

"Luc has never been the talkative type," Juliet replied. "He's not one to share his deepest feelings easily. That's not to say that he doesn't have heartfelt emotions, he does even if he doesn't always want to. But he believes that emotions get in the way."

The dowager queen nodded her approval. "A proper royal attitude to be sure."

Juliet boldly gathered her courage. "I hope you won't try and change Luc. He needs the freedom to be himself."

The dowager queen gave an imperial shrug. "A certain amount of freedom is lost when you are of royal birth, there is no getting around that fact."

"I realize that. But I'd hate to see Luc turn into an emotionless and distant man. I don't want that for him."

"What *do* you want for him?"

"His happiness," Juliet said simply. "I just want him to be happy."

"Ah, that may be harder to achieve than you think."

"I'd do anything in my power to make him happy," Juliet fiercely vowed.

"Would you now, child? That's admirable." The dowager queen's smile turned slightly melancholy. "But I fear that making Luc happy may be something that is beyond either of our abilities to control."

Juliet flopped down on her bed with a sigh of relief. She'd survived tea with the dowager queen. Not only had she survived but she'd struck gold—coming back with several pages of notes about the older woman's life, including her recollections of her mother and herself as a young woman accompanying the royal family to London, where they lived in exile throughout the 1940s and the worst of the Second World War.

At the time, St. Michel had an active resistance movement, like the French Resistance, and most of the men of the aristocracy joined forces with their fellow countrymen. King Philippe's grandmother had carried top secret messages with her to give to the British authorities. Another case of a royal de Bergeron woman stepping forward to act courageously.

A sudden pounding on her door interrupted her thoughts. She was surprised to find Luc standing in the hallway. Looking sexy and agitated, he strode past her without even waiting for an invitation to come in. Juliet barely closed the door before he began speaking. "I heard you were commanded to appear before the dowager queen."

"She invited me to tea."

"What for? Did she try and pump you for information about me? What did you tell her?"

She put her finger on his lips as he'd once done her. "One question at a time. Do you remember when we had that protocol lesson in the dining room? When I talked about the difference between interrogation and conversation? This would be a prime example. You're interrogating me."

"I most certainly am." He relaxed his tense stance and began seductively nibbling her finger. "And I make no apologies for that."

"For what?" Her voice was breathless and distracted.

"For interrogating you. I'm attempting to get the facts here."

"And did you think you could nibble them out of me?" She would have sounded righteously indignant were it not for the hint of laughter in her voice.

"I thought it might be fun to find out."

Fun? That was putting it mildly.

"So what did the dowager queen want?"

Juliet couldn't speak coherently and be seduced by him at the same time.

Taking a step away from him allowed her to resist the temptation Luc provided. "She said she wanted to get to know me better."

"She's known you for years. You came to live here at the palace when you were what—four?"

"We spent most summers and many vacations with my father's family so that my mother could focus on bearing Philippe a son. When I was here, I tried to be as quiet and inconspicuous as possible so I wouldn't be sent away again. Not that we didn't have a wonderful time with my father's family, we did. But I missed my mother when I was away from her.''

"Of course you did. That's no way for a child to be treated.''

"You weren't treated the way a child should be treated, either, being sent off to boarding school so young.''

"Something we both have in common, eh?'' He brushed his fingers across her cheek while gazing at her with his rich blue eyes. "Mothers who selfishly went after what they wanted and damn the consequences.''

"Or mothers who thought they were doing what was best for us in a difficult situation.'' She captured his hand and held it in hers. "Have you thought about reading the letter your mother left you?''

"I've thought about it.''

"And?''

"And I'm not doing it. Don't give me that look. There's nothing she can say that would change what she did.''

"I agree that nothing can change *what* she did, but her letter might explain *why* she did it.''

"You've always got an answer to everything, don't you?''

"I just want what's best for you, Luc.''

"This is what's best for me,'' he murmured lowering his head to brush his lips over hers. "Being with you.''

She felt a ripple of anticipation slide up her spine as he tasted and tested the corners of her mouth, sliding across the full softness in between before lingering. The kiss grew and expanded from one delicious caress into an intimate seduction. Lost in the intimacies of his tongue moving against hers, she was further enthralled by the passage of his hands over her body.

The demure floral dress she'd worn to the dowager queen's tea was turned into a temptress's gown in his able hands. The soft cotton material magnified his every caress, allowing her to feel each one of his fingers as they glided from her back to her breast.

His embrace became a passport to a world of wondrous sensations as he teased the roof of her mouth with his tongue and claimed her breast in the palm of his hand, his fingers closing over her warm and willing flesh. He brushed her firm nipple with his thumb, making her burn with forbidden pleasure.

Her knees became weak, and she welcomed the feel of a soft mattress beneath her. His lips never left hers as he followed her down, blanketing her with his powerful body.

Rolling onto his side, he pulled her closer. She melted against him, caught up in the magic of his touch.

His knowing fingers gained entrance to the front fastening of her bra. Her highly sensitized nerve endings vibrated when she felt his warm breath on her now-bare skin. Luc didn't hurry as he caressed and nibbled, kissed and paid homage to every delectable inch of her breasts—running his tongue from the upper line of her ribs to nuzzle the firm underside. Then he traveled up and over, his evocative tongue wickedly trailing along, following the passage of faint blue veins against the creaminess of her flesh until he reached the sensitive peak. His thumb ventured closer, guiding her into the warmth of his mouth.

Juliet moaned with pleasure and arched her back. His wet heat surrounded even more of her now, even as his lower body throbbed against hers. The hard ridge beneath his trousers fitted with exquisite precision against the aching secret juncture of her body. The stroking contact was more arousing and exciting than anything she'd ever known before.

The temptation to experience the full possession of this man, to be just once wholly his, was overwhelming. As he settled even more of his weight over her, she greedily welcomed him—his powerful body, his creative seduction. She wanted more.

He slid his fingers beneath her dress, caressing the back of her knee before moving upward to her thigh and increasingly closer to the one spot that wept with need. By now the friction of his body moving against hers had become a delicious torment, one he huskily promised to remedy.

Passion prevailed as her mind was completely monopolized by her body's urgent desire to merge with his, for the two of them to become one. Urging him on, she opened herself to him.

But before his seductive fingers could gain access, they were interrupted by the arrival of thirty-six sharp claws scrambling across their partially clothed bodies.

"Ouch!" Luc exclaimed.

"Be careful, it's the kittens," she warned him, fearing he might toss them aside. "Don't hurt them."

"I would never hurt them, but they can't say the same for me." He held out his arm, which now showed a bright red scratch on it.

"I'm so sorry. I know I'm not supposed to have the kittens in the palace, but I was afraid Mittens and Rascal would get trampled by the horses if I left them in the stables. So I sneaked them inside yesterday." Juliet stopped her self-conscious refastening of her clothing to gaze at him. "I'm so sorry they hurt you. Shall I kiss it better?"

His eyes met hers, and he spoke to her without saying a word, making her breath catch and her heart race. The undisguised passion she saw reflected in their blue depths was overwhelming. His gaze ranged over her now-covered curves with the erotic knowledge of a man who'd touched her intimately, who'd taken her to the very threshold of passion's gate.

Her body still vibrated with that awareness.

Before Luc could speak or act on the fiery desire etched on his face, they were interrupted again as the door bounced open. This time it wasn't kittens, it was her younger sister Jacqueline.

"So, what are you two up to...or shouldn't I ask?" the precocious adolescent inquired with a wicked grin.

Chapter Nine

"**J**acqueline!" Juliet leapt from the bed as if propelled by one of the medieval catapults on display in the palace dungeon. "What are you doing here? And why is your hair purple?"

"More important what are you and Luc doing on your bed?"

"Nothing." Juliet frantically smoothed her hair, which had come loose from the French braid. "I was just showing him the kittens."

"I don't think that's all you were showing him," her impudent sister drawled.

Juliet frowned at her. "I thought you wouldn't be back until next week."

"I missed everyone in St. Michel too much to stay away any longer."

"Well, I'd better get back to work." Luc was clearly eager to avoid getting stuck overhearing a sisterly heart-to-heart conversation.

"You might want to wipe the lipstick from your cheek before you do," Jacqueline advised him.

"She's just kidding," Juliet hastily assured Luc. "There is no lipstick on your cheek."

Jacqueline showed no remorse. "Only because my bookish big sister doesn't wear any."

"Nice having you back, Muffin," Luc told her with a grin.

"Nice being back, Spyman." Seeing Juliet's startled look, the twelve-year-old added, "That's my nickname for him. Didn't you tell her, Luc?"

He shook his head, which tumbled more of his dark hair onto his forehead. Had she messed up his hair? Juliet had hazy memories of running her fingers through the surprisingly silky dark strands as he caressed her bare breasts with his seductive mouth and tongue.

"No, I didn't tell her," Luc was saying. "Some things are meant to be top secret, Muffin."

Jacqueline nodded with a maturity beyond her years. "Understood, Spyman. See you around."

Juliet waited until Luc had left before turning to her sister. "Jacqueline, you really can't go calling Luc Spyman any longer."

"Why not?"

"Because...well..." She floundered a moment, remembering that Luc didn't want anyone else knowing about his true background just yet. "I can't tell you all the details right now, but believe me when I say that there are very good reasons."

"You mean because he may soon be king?"

Juliet almost swallowed her tongue. "Where did you hear that?"

Jacqueline shrugged and dropped into a nearby comfy

chair, flinging one leg over the arm. "Grandmama told me. I stopped by to see her before coming here."

The dowager queen was indeed Jacqueline's grandmother. Her sister was able to straddle both worlds—the royal world of her father the king and the real world of their mother. All this and she was only twelve.

Still stunned, Juliet was not expecting her sister's next observation. "So, Luc has turned out to be quite a hottie, huh?"

Juliet blushed a brilliant shade of red.

"Oh, so you think so, too?" Her sister practically chortled with delight.

"I think that purple hair better be temporary. And you should have changed clothes before seeing the dowager queen." Juliet tugged her sister to her feet. "Why are there holes in your jeans? That top is much too skimpy. And what is that in your navel?"

"It's not permanent. It's a navel gem. And the girls at school love my clothes, they think I look like Britney Spears."

"Not a goal of mine, I admit. And it shouldn't be one of yours, either. She is an entertainer, you are—"

"The daughter of a king," Jacqueline cut in. "Yeah, I've heard it all before. And for your information, Grandmama loved my outfit. And my hair. She told me so herself. She said if she were a decade or two younger, she'd be wearing a navel gem herself."

Juliet had to laugh at the idea of the proper dowager queen ever showing her navel.

"You should show more skin yourself," Jacqueline advised her. "You usually dress as if you were Grandmama's age."

"Thank you for those kind words," Juliet noted dryly.

"I wasn't trying to be insulting, I was just telling the

truth. Isn't that what you are always after me to do? To tell the truth?''

"When it's appropriate.''

"And when it's not?'' Jacqueline instantly demanded.

"Then if you can't say something nice, say nothing at all.''

"I like your kittens. That's something nice, isn't it?'' She scooped Rascal up and dropped back into the chair. "So tell me, why were you and Luc making out?''

"Jacqueline!''

Her younger sister blinked up at her, making Juliet realize that she was wearing glittery eyeshadow that matched her purple hair. "What?''

"That is not an appropriate question. Not that Luc and I were making out.'' First lying to the dowager queen earlier that afternoon, now lying to her sister. What was happening to her? Juliet wondered. She used to be a very honest person, wrapped up in her books and research. Not at all the kind of woman who'd make out with a sexy man like Luc.

"Now who's not telling the truth?'' Jacqueline sent a very pointed look at the rumpled bedcoverings.

Juliet was about to resume her defensive posture when an inner voice advised her to wait a minute. Her younger sister was not her keeper. Juliet was the older, the wiser, and the more conservative one. Usually. "I don't have to explain myself to you.''

"Why not?'' Jacqueline's mutinous expression was pure adolescence. At times like this, Juliet fervently wished their mother was still alive to help guide them both. "I always have to tell you everything. It's not fair.''

"Life isn't always fair,'' Juliet noted quietly. "I suppose it's time we both learned that.''

* * *

"Ah, Luc, I'm so glad you decided to join us," the dowager queen said as she welcomed him to the White Drawing Room.

Luc knew this was the room where the dowager queen had hosted tea with Juliet earlier that afternoon, before he'd almost seduced Juliet in her own bed. His body still hadn't recovered. He was a man accustomed to being in control—of his life, of his future, of his emotions. All that had been blown sky-high the past few weeks and he was left with chaos. He did not like chaos.

This was neither the time nor the place to brood over what had happened—not to mention what had almost happened—in Juliet's private apartments. His thoughts were too jumbled to make any sense at the moment anyway.

"I'm joining you because you practically ordered me here."

"You're the king." She gave him an arch look. "No one should be able to order you to do anything."

"That's the first good thing I've heard about this job," he growled. "So what's the emergency?"

"You do have a way of getting right to the point, don't you?" She didn't make it sound like a compliment, and her laser gaze indicated her displeasure.

"So I've been told."

"By Juliet?"

"You and I had an agreement about my private life being off-limits, remember?"

"We had an agreement that you would call me Grandmother, remember? And that you would spend more time with me."

Luc sighed. "I spent time with you yesterday morning, Grandmother. That's when you promised not to interfere in my private life, remember?"

"I promised not to interrogate you again. I didn't say anything about not interrogating Juliet. But that's besides the point. I called you here today to discuss St. Michel's national security."

"Then why isn't the prime minister here?"

"The poor man came down with a touch of tummy flu. Too many hours spent with the Privy Council if you ask me."

"What is this matter of national security you're talking about?"

"I think Ariane and Etienne should tell you themselves. Ah, here they are now. Right on time."

Prince Etienne of Rhineland had the aristocratic bearing of a man born into royalty. Wearing a superbly tailored suit, he possessed the confidence of a ruler.

Not that Luc wasn't a confident man. He was. But a ruler? The jury was still out on that one.

Like her husband, Princess Ariane also had that regal manner down pat. A petite woman with blond shoulder-length hair and blue eyes, she had an adventurous nature that sometimes got her into trouble. For instance, there had been the time she'd decided to go to Rhineland to spy on the royal family in an attempt to learn more about the rumored plot to take over St. Michel. She'd learned that the royal family had no part in it, and then she'd fallen in love with the prince.

To his surprise, Ariane came right up to him and hugged him. She grinned at his stunned expression. "It's so good to see you again, Luc. I've always wanted a big brother."

Luc glared at the dowager queen who merely smiled back at him. "I thought we agreed not to tell anyone," he reminded his grandmother.

"Ariane isn't *anyone*. She's my granddaughter."

Luc shot a look at Etienne, who merely rolled his eyes as if to say it's no use fighting these two.

"Is that why you called for me?" Luc demanded. "Because Ariane is here for a visit?"

"Because she and Etienne have something important to tell you."

"We have news regarding the extremist faction known as Rhinelanders for Annexation, or RFA," Etienne said.

Luc nodded. "I'm familiar with the organization."

"We've long suspected they had a plan to overthrow the monarch and the government here and annex St. Michel to Rhineland. As you know, my family does not approve of any such move and has made an official statement to that effect. But this group is very good at playing on the strong nationalistic feelings of my countrymen. They excel at bringing out the worst in people."

"I'm familiar with that type of modus operandi." In his years at Interpol, Luc had dealt with various extremist groups who took violent action to have their agendas met.

"We arrested two of the group's leaders several weeks ago, but suspected that they were merely the front men for the organization. We had no idea who was really pulling the strings."

"And supplying the money," Ariane added.

"A great deal of money," Etienne agreed. "We just arrested Berg Dekker when he returned to Rhineland earlier this morning."

"Berg Dekker?" Luc shook his head in amazement. "I've heard of him, of course. He's a frequent target of the regional environmental groups because of his practices." Luc had long wondered how Dekker got approval to use St. Michel River to ship his petroleum products to and from the North Sea. Other European countries had turned him down, citing his poor record in abiding by local shipping restrictions and his goal of putting profits above all else.

Luc had never been in a position to question Dekker's business dealings before. It was just hitting him that he now was. "What do you have on Dekker?"

"Our authorities have been following an elaborate paper trail of hidden trusts and dummy corporations, following the money that Dekker took in and where it went. He illegally funneled a lot of it into the Rhinelanders for Annexation group. We also uncovered his plot to destabilize the economy of Rhineland to unseat the monarchy so that he could run as the country's savior."

"How does this affect St. Michel?" Luc asked.

"Luc is a bottom-line sort of man," the dowager queen said apologetically.

He glared at her. It stung his pride to have someone apologizing for his behavior.

"That's what will make him such a great king," Ariane declared. "He'll cut through all the cow dung and get right to business."

"Ariane!" The dowager queen fixed her with a disapproving look before cracking a slight smile. "A royal does not refer to cow dung."

Ariane was not intimidated. "Would you prefer I call it by one of its more vulgar names?"

"I'd prefer you not mention it at all. Now where were we? Ah, yes, Etienne, you were about to tell us more about how this Dekker fellow relates to St. Michel."

"In addition to his plot to destabilize Rhineland, he also planned to move forward and annex St. Michel. At least that was his plan until he met with Queen Celeste."

"He met with Queen Celeste?"

"So he claims. We have no proof that the meeting took

place. But Dekker swears that Celeste came to him with an offer."

"I knew that woman was a hussy!" the dowager queen declared.

"Not a sexual offer," Etienne quickly clarified. "A business offer. Dekker says she promised him unlimited access to the St. Michel River in exchange for his supporting her infant son's claim to the throne."

"Of all the nerve!"

"Now, Grandmother…"

"We have no proof," Etienne reminded them. "Celeste denies the meeting ever took place. She claims that Dekker is merely trying to make trouble for her, to destabilize St. Michel just as he planned to destabilize Rhineland."

"I don't believe a word she says," Ariane declared. "Etienne and I came here today to warn you, Luc. To warn you about Celeste. She clearly plans on doing whatever it takes to put her baby son on the throne. Perhaps it's time to tell her you are the rightful heir."

"If she's as devious as you say she is, then she probably already knows. Which is why…"

"Why what?" Ariane asked.

"Nothing." Luc shook his head. "It's just that Juliet was suspicious of a few strange occurrences."

"What kind of strange occurrences?" Ariane demanded.

Luc briefly told them about the falling gargoyle and the collapsing tent at the carnival. "Clearly not the work of a professional. If Celeste wanted me dead, there are definitely more effective ways of trying to assassinate me."

"Don't underestimate her," Ariane warned him. "Just

because she's been foolish so far doesn't mean she won't turn deadly at the drop of a hat."

"Or the drop of a crown. There's a lot at stake for her," Etienne said. "I agree with my lovely wife. Don't underestimate Celeste."

"They've arrested Dekker!" Claude entered Celeste's riverfront apartment and then collapsed on her red velvet settee.

"Do stop hyperventilating, Claude."

"Didn't you hear me? Dekker was arrested the moment he returned to Rhineland this morning. It's on all the news reports. They're saying that he tried to overthrow the government."

"What government?"

"In Rhineland."

"Then we're fine. We're not involved with the government of Rhineland."

"No, but we just negotiated a deal with Dekker a few days ago. He's bound to tell the authorities that."

"He has. And I've already denied it." She studied her perfectly manicured nails before giving Claude a reprimanding stare. "You really should learn not to panic. It's not an admirable trait by any means."

"How could I not panic? The man we made an illegal deal with was just arrested."

"There was nothing illegal about our deal with him. And even if there was, no one else need know about it. The main problem here is Luc."

"Luc?" Claude was clearly bewildered.

"Do try and keep up," she told him tartly. "Luc is about to be named heir to the throne. We can't let that happen."

"So we're back to the plan of killing him?"

Celeste sighed. "It would appear so."

* * *

"So how does this royalty thing work?" Luc voiced the question from his office chair.

"Pretty well from my perspective," Etienne answered from the chair across the room.

They'd spent the past few hours reviewing the case against Dekker, going over the intelligence files Etienne had brought with him from Rhineland. Then Luc had brought out a bottle of fine brandy and the discussion had grown a bit more personal.

"Yes, well you were born into the job, so to speak. And speaking of jobs, I suppose I'm going to have to find a new head of security soon. Damn." Luc rubbed his forehead. "I really liked this job, this office."

"You could move the throne in here."

"The dowager queen would have a fit."

"She's more resilient than you think."

"It's not her resilience I'm worried about, it's mine." Luc jumped up and started pacing. "How do you manage to have a private life? You married a princess. But what about someone outside of the royalty business?"

"Wait a moment, marrying Ariane was anything but a no-brainer. We certainly had more than our fair share of troubles."

"Yes, but she *is* a princess. She, like you, grew up in this world."

"Are you talking about marrying a commoner?"

"I'm not talking about marriage at all."

"Then what are you talking about?"

"Damned if I know," Luc muttered, walking over to his window to stare down at the fountain where he'd kissed Juliet.

"Do you have a certain woman in mind?"

"All the time. She's in my mind all the time."

"And you don't think she'd be someone suitable?"

"She's very suitable. For me, Luc. But she wouldn't just be getting involved with me. She'd be getting involved with the King of St. Michel."

"Involved but not married?"

"I don't know." Luc shoved his free hand through his hair before taking another healthy swig of brandy. "I can't seem to think very straight these days."

"I've had almost thirty years to become accustomed to my title," Etienne said. "You've had what…a few weeks? Give yourself time."

"I've run out of time. The dowager queen told me tonight that the Privy Council will be approving my claim to the throne within the next forty-eight hours or less."

"Not much time left to get your thoughts in order."

When Etienne left a short while later, Luc returned to his desk, intending to clear up some outstanding paperwork. If someone else was going to take over this job, then he wanted everything in tip-top shape when they came in. Someone else sitting in his chair, at his desk. The thought irked him.

Maybe he should bring the pieces of furniture with him to wherever it was that the king did his daily job. Luc wasn't even sure what room in the palace it was. He should know that. As head of security, he no doubt did know it at one time. A time when he'd been a sane man with a fairly normal background. Until this king thing.

He snapped another file folder closed, and, as he did so, something caught on the edge of the paper before slipping to the floor. Picking it up, he realized that it was the letter from his mother. Juliet must have left it here that morning she'd come to perch so seductively on the corner of his desk, the morning he'd first asked her to help him by giving him lessons on how to be a king.

Read it Luc. He could almost hear Juliet's voice. *Read the letter.*

He tore open the envelope.

To My Dearest Son,

If you're reading this letter it means Albert has already told you the facts about your heritage. I need to tell you the *reasons,* to tell you why I had to deceive you.

I know you're probably angry with me for never telling you who your biological father was, but I didn't want you saddled with the stigma of illegitimacy. When Philippe's parents told me that the marriage wasn't valid because I was underage, something inside me just crumbled and withered. Perhaps I should have been stronger, perhaps I should have done things differently.

I can only say that I have always loved you, from the second the nurses put you in my arms. Know that you are and always will be my beloved son, the light of my life. And please forgive me.

                                        Your loving mother.

The last few words were a bit smeared, as if they'd got wet at one point. Had his mother cried as she wrote the letter?

Something inside him, an invisible inner wall, cracked—allowing a trickle of emotion through. His fingers clenched around his empty brandy glass as he stared at the letter until his eyes burned. *My dearest son…you are and always will be my beloved son…your loving mother.* The words shifted and blurred.

A muscle in his jaw clenched. His mother had died without ever knowing her marriage to Philippe was indeed legal. The injustice of it all hit him with the power of a fist.

"Luc?"

For one fleeting instant, he thought the tentative woman's voice was that of his mother. He blinked before identifying her. The dowager queen.

"Are you all right?" She came forward into his office.

"Why?" He drilled her with his fierce gaze. "Why did you tell my mother the marriage wasn't valid?"

"Ah." She slipped into a nearby chair, looking as old as her years for the first time. "I was wondering when that would hit you."

"She left me a letter."

"I see." Her face seemed to age even more. "And did she curse me in it?"

"No." Luc's harsh voice caught. "She asked me to forgive her."

"And do you?"

He paused a moment before nodding. He could forgive his mother now that he'd read her words.

"Good. But now you're not sure about forgiving me, correct?"

"Correct."

"Ah, Luc. I wish I could tell you how it was. Katie's father was only a middle-management employee of an American corporation. They had no money and no social standing. Three decades ago, that was a major thing. Her father was here in St. Michel on business for three months. Katie had plenty of time to explore the area. She met my son, and they fell in love. She became pregnant, and, without telling anyone beforehand, they went to France and were secretly married in a civil ceremony.

My husband, King Antoine, told Philippe that the marriage wasn't valid because Katie was only seventeen. I didn't know whether that was true or not. But in my mind, King Antoine was the absolute ruler, the final word on any subject. If he said it wasn't valid, it wasn't valid. King Antoine also informed Katie's father that if they told anyone about this scandalous affair, he would pressure her father's employer to fire him. The king gave Katie's father a substantial sum of money, without her consent or approval. I'll never forget the look on her face as her father whisked her away.''

The dowager queen had to pause to regain her composure before continuing. ''Do I wish that we hadn't interfered in our son's life? Without a shadow of a doubt. I believe that Philippe spent the rest of his life trying to find the kind of love he shared with Katie and that he went to his grave loving her.'' Her voice trembled with emotion. ''I wish we had brought Katie home to the palace with us, that I'd been there to hold you when you were born, to lavish you with attention as I did my granddaughters while they were growing up. But I wasn't. I can't undo the past, Luc. I can only look ahead to the future. Your future. The King of St. Michel's future.'' She held out her thin elegant hand, wrinkled with age. That's when Luc realized that the lavish diamond King Antoine had given her was no longer sparkling on her left finger.

''Where's your ring?'' His voice sounded rusty even to his own ears.

''I put it in the vault. I no longer choose to remain tied to my husband and the bad choices he made and I went along with. I want to make a new start. Granted, seventy-something might be a tad late to start fresh, but I'm game if you are. What about it, Luc? You told me that I should try asking instead of ordering. So here I am.'' Her outstretched hand trembled and her laser-blue eyes were filled with deep-seated pain and uncertainty. "Asking...no...*begging* you for forgiveness and the chance to start anew.''

Luc took her hand in his. A second later he was around the desk, kneeling before her with his arms around her surprisingly slight frame.

"Welcome home, my boy.'' He could almost hear his mother's voice repeating his grandmother's refrain. *Welcome home, Luc. Welcome home, my dearest son.*

Chapter Ten

Juliet was up with the sun the next morning, taking an early-morning walk in the palace gardens to clear her mind. She hadn't been able to sleep much at all last night. The erotic memory of Luc's lovemaking had kept her awake—her body still thrumming from the unresolved passion of their heated embrace.

She'd always been a firm believer in waiting until after marriage before giving her virginity to the man she loved. That resolve had never been tested before, not even with Armand. But Luc was different. He had a way of overwhelming her common sense and going right to her heart.

The fact that she was intensely attracted to him wasn't the reason they'd almost made love yesterday. Hormones alone didn't rule her actions, *love* did. And that potent combination had proven too powerful to resist.

What would have happened if the kittens and her sister hadn't interrupted them? Would Luc have made love with her? Did he know she was a virgin? Would that matter to him? It wasn't anything they'd ever discussed, not being a topic that was easy to include in everyday conversation.

Juliet had no doubt that Luc was accustomed to women with more sexual experience than she had. But that hadn't seemed to bother him yesterday. He'd groaned with pleasure when she'd returned his kisses. His hard body had throbbed with desire for her. His voice had been husky with need as he'd whispered in her ear, and his blue eyes had blazed down at her with smoldering passion.

The memory alone was enough to make her weak at the knees. As she sank onto one of the rustic benches lining the winding path, she tried to distract herself by focusing on her surroundings. It promised to be another gorgeous late-spring day, with only a few billowy cumulus clouds to add a bit of interest to an otherwise intensely blue sky. Not the blue of Luc's eyes, however. They were darker than sky blue. She'd long ago given up trying to put an exact color on them—they were simply his eyes and they were awesome because they were *his*.

Her gaze wandered over the gardens themselves. The irises were almost through blooming and the rest of the roses were about to burst into color. With their fragrant blossoms and beautiful displays, they were a favorite of hers. Climbing roses in a delicious shade of apricot clambered alongside deep purple clematis over the ten-foot arbor surrounding her.

It was so peaceful here. Birds chirped as they hopped from branch to branch on a nearby tree. A huge bumblebee droned lazily right over her head as it meandered from flower to flower. Then Juliet heard something else, something not as serene as the natural symphony of the birds and the breeze rustling through the leaves. It sounded like someone softly sobbing.

Juliet left the arbor and followed the heartwrenching noise to the back end of the garden. There she found Yvette, the head gardener's wife, sobbing while attempting to till the small vegetable garden beside the gardener's house. Her infant was apparently sleeping in a wicker bassinet on the bench by the back door.

"What is it, Yvette?" Juliet put an arm around her trembling shoulders. "What's wrong?"

The other woman kept crying.

"Is it the baby?"

Yvette's crying increased.

Alarmed, Juliet said, "I'll go fetch the royal physician."

"No!" Yvette stopped her sobbing to grab Juliet's arm with desperate hands. "No, you mustn't."

"If the baby is sick, then we have to have a doctor check her out."

"She's not sick."

"Then what's wrong? You've been acting strangely for days now, Yvette. I've heard about postpartum depression caused by the hormonal changes after pregnancy. Why don't we have the physician check you out just to be sure?"

Yvette wiped the tears from her cheeks and stared at Juliet with a miserable expression in her brown eyes. "I know what's wrong with me and it has nothing to do with hormones."

"Then what is it? You know you can trust me, Yvette."

"I don't know what to do." Yvette plucked at her apron. "I swore I wouldn't tell anyone ever, but I can't live with what I've done."

"Is it your husband?" Juliet prompted gently. "Your marriage?"

"I didn't want to do it." Yvette's tears started to roll again. "I told my husband that it was wrong, that no amount of money could make up for what we had done."

Juliet patted her on the back sympathetically. "Go on."

"My husband's mother is ill and needed expensive medical treatment available here in St. Michel. The debts began to mount. That's when she came to us. With an offer."

"Who came to you?"

"Queen Celeste. Or rather one of her representatives."

"A man or woman?"

"A man. Dr. Mellion."

Juliet had never liked Celeste's physician. He had an arrogant way about him.

Yvette continued. "He presented us with an offer, enough money to pay for all the medical bills and much more as well."

"In exchange for what?"

"For my baby." Yvette whispered the words.

Juliet was stunned. "He wanted to buy your baby daughter?"

"No, he wanted to buy my baby son."

Now Juliet was confused. "But you ended up having a girl."

Yvette nervously looked over her shoulder. "Perhaps I shouldn't be telling you any of this."

"Most definitely you should tell me everything," Juliet stated firmly. "Did the doctor say why he wanted to buy your baby?"

"It was only in the event that Queen Celeste had a baby girl."

"But she had a boy and you had the girl. So the deal fell through, right?"

Yvette shook her head, her short dark curly hair bouncing in the slight breeze. "No, it did not fall through. I wish it had. I wish with all my heart that it had. But it did not."

"What do you mean? What are you saying, Yvette?"

"That I sold my baby boy to the queen."

"And the baby girl you have?"

"Is the queen's," Yvette confessed in a hushed, frightened voice.

"But how…?"

"Dr. Mellion switched the babies shortly after they were born. When it was discovered that Queen Celeste had given birth to a daughter, her doctor and his assistant came and took my son. I'd given birth a few hours before. I barely had time to see him, to hold him before he was taken from me. Ripped from my arms. I begged them not to take him." Tears streamed down Yvette's flushed cheeks. "But they took him anyway. They gave me a baby girl instead."

Juliet was stunned by this news. She'd always known that Celeste was a schemer but she'd never expected her to go this far, to steal another woman's baby and try to pass it off as her own. The suspicions had been that perhaps the child wasn't really the king's, that it was the result of a liaison with a lover. But no one had suspected that Celeste wasn't the mother. That was too wild a scenario for anyone to have come up with. Anyone but Celeste.

"Oh, Yvette." Juliet hugged her. "I'm so sorry that they put you through this."

"We made a bargain with the devil, it is right that we pay. But it isn't right that these two innocent babies pay as well. I want my son back."

"I know you do. Don't worry, we'll get him back for

you. There now, dry your tears. We'll go to Luc and tell him everything. He'll take it from there."

"We'll be sent to jail." Yvette's voice trembled with fear.

"No, you won't. The doctor may well go to jail, but you won't."

"But I sold my baby."

"It was not your idea. Your husband agreed to the plan because he was in dire need of money for his poor sick mother. No one will blame him for that, although they may question his judgment in agreeing to this plan. But it is Celeste and the doctor who are to blame here. They are the ones who initiated this devious plan."

"You really think we can get my little boy back without going to jail?" For the first time, a faint glimmer of hope shone in her dark eyes.

"I'm certain of it. Come now, dry those tears." Juliet paused at the sound of her name being urgently called. "Here, I'm here."

Henri, one of the footmen, came rushing into the vegetable garden, crushing the tender vegetation beneath his feet. "We have been searching for you everywhere, Miss Juliet. You must come at once. There has been an accident."

The hairs on the back of her neck prickled and she went cold all over. "An accident?"

"Yes. It's Luc Dumont. He's asking for you. I was told to bring you to him immediately. Come, we mustn't wait. Every second counts!"

"What happened? How badly is he hurt?"

"The injuries are serious," Henri replied. "Life-threatening."

Juliet's heart stopped. She couldn't breathe. Luc, seriously hurt. It was her worst nightmare come true. Talons of panic clawed their way through her.

"You, there." Henri pointed at Yvette. "I fear Miss Juliet is going to need comforting when she sees how badly off Luc is. You must accompany us."

"But I can't leave the baby," Yvette protested.

"Bring the infant with us," Henri said, "but hurry. Or we shall be too late. There's a car waiting to take you to him."

Dazed and terrified for Luc, Juliet nodded for Yvette to do as Henri said. Moments later they were in a dark sedan rushing from the palace. It was only then that she realized they weren't alone in the sedan. Claude Guignard, St. Michel's deputy energy minister, was in the car with them. He patted her hand with commiseration. "It doesn't look good. I'm sorry."

"Were you with Luc? What can you tell me about the accident?"

"There was an explosion. I was sent to get you."

Please God, let him live. Don't let him die!

Juliet kept repeating that prayer over and over again, as they raced through the city of St. Michel. "Wait, your driver missed the turnoff to the hospital."

"Luc isn't at the hospital."

"Why not?"

"He was injured near the warehouses down by the river. They fear moving him before his condition has been stabilized. To do so would guarantee his death."

Cold terror gripped every part of her body, making it hard for her even to breathe.

What had Luc been doing at a warehouse by the river? Had he been following a lead about the Rhinelanders for Annexation group? Had they caused his accident? St. Michel had never had to worry about terrorist activities in the past, but the world was a different place these days. If the deputy energy minister was involved, then it must have something to do with petroleum? At one of the loading facilities along the river perhaps?

"We'll be there in a minute or two," Claude assured her.

True to his word, the sedan pulled to a halt beside one of the warehouses. Juliet was out of the car in an instant. "Hurry! Take me to Luc!"

"Follow me." Claude led them inside.

The difference between the bright sunshine outside and the darkness of the warehouse had Juliet pausing for a moment as she frantically tried to scan the room. "I don't see him, Mr. Guignard. Where is he?"

"In the small storeroom ahead." He stood aside to let them go ahead of him.

Juliet and Yvette had no sooner stepped into the room than the door was slammed behind them.

The light in there was even dimmer, provided only by a small and dingy barred window located up near the ceiling. There was no sign of Luc, or of anyone else.

Juliet was getting a very bad feeling about this. She turned to the closed door. "Mr. Guignard, open the door." She was rather proud of the command in her voice, using her best dowager queen impersonation. "Open the door this instant!"

"I'm afraid I can't do that, Juliet."

The baby started to cry.

It was all a ruse. Juliet realized that now. "Luc isn't hurt at all, is he? You said that to get me here. Why?"

"Because I overheard Yvette spilling her heart to you, the stupid fool. I had to do something before you went to Luc and told him everything."

"Now, Claude, you don't want to do this." Her voice

was more empathetic now. Obviously the commanding stuff hadn't worked. Besides, it wasn't a natural for her. "You're not thinking clearly."

"Of course I'm not thinking clearly!" he shouted in return, making the baby cry all the more. Yvette was also starting to sob quietly.

Juliet refused to give in to fear or panic. Too late, she recalled rumors linking Claude with Celeste. "You can't just keep us locked up here."

"I can and I will until I figure out what to do next. Don't bother screaming, both warehouses on either side are deserted this time of year. No one will hear you."

"Luc will come after me. He'll find us."

"No, he won't." Claude's voice sounded dangerously confident. "I'll make sure of that."

The door to the White Drawing Room swung open and bounced against the wall. Luc automatically assumed a defensive posture. He never sat in a room with his back to the door, part of his security training. When he saw it was only Jacqueline, he relaxed. Then he tensed up again at the possibility that the precocious adolescent had come to tell his grandmother about finding Luc and Juliet together on her bed yesterday afternoon.

He tried to read the girl's expression, but all he got was panic. Which meant what? In Jacqueline's case it could mean anything from a clothing crisis to a rumor about one of her favorite boy bands calling it quits. She looked like something from an MTV video with her denim miniskirt and her stretchy top covering only one shoulder. And then there was her purple hair.

"A princess never runs into a room as if she were on

fire, *mignon*," the dowager queen reprimanded her. "I've told you that before."

"Have you seen Juliet?" Jacqueline's chest was heaving as if she'd been running. It made the sparkling blue gem in her navel dip and ripple.

"No," the dowager queen replied, not the least bit flustered by her granddaughter's garish appearance.

"She's missing!" Jacqueline exclaimed.

The dowager queen wasn't impressed. "What are you talking about? You really must curb that dramatic streak of yours, Jacqueline."

But Luc took her words seriously. "When was the last time you saw her?"

"Last night. She left a note on my door at six this morning saying she was going to go for a walk in the gardens. That was hours ago."

Luc was instantly on alert. "Have you had the guards check the gardens?"

Jacqueline nodded. "Yes, and I've checked the palace as well. She's not in her office or her quarters. And none of the servants have seen her, either. Alistair already asked everyone."

"Did you check the stables? There were kittens there…"

"I checked. No one there has seen her at all today."

"I'm sure she's fine," the dowager queen said.

"Then where is she?"

"Come on, I'll help you find her," Luc said.

"But, Luc!" the dowager queen protested. "What about Celeste? You are supposed to be going to an emergency meeting with the prime minister about the situation."

Luc's reply was curt. "Celeste and the prime minister can both wait. Juliet is more important."

"What other songs do you know, Yvette?" Juliet stood perched on an overturned storage box as she tried to reach the tiny window. This was one of the few times she was glad of her height. Just a few inches more and she'd be able to at least look outside, see if anyone was about. Meanwhile, she needed Yvette to keep making noise as she joined her in loud choruses of everything from Broadway show tunes to French lullabies to Madonna's songs. There was always a chance that some passerby might hear them. Screaming for help for almost an hour had only increased their panic and left their voices hoarse. That's when Juliet had come up with the singing idea.

"I can't sing any longer, miss."

"Certainly you can. You mustn't give up, Yvette."

"We are doomed!" the other woman wailed. "Didn't you hear them talking about us? That man plans on putting us in the cargo hold of some river barge and shipping us off to South Africa. I'll never see my baby boy again."

"Now, Yvette…"

"They're going to win! They're going to kill Luc and have my son take over as the ruling king. Queen Celeste is going to win."

"Stop that." Juliet jumped down from her makeshift ladder to grab Yvette by the shoulders. "Look at me. And listen to me. No one is going to hurt Luc. He's had years of training as a security specialist. He knows what he's doing. He will find us. And until he does, we have to stay calm and be smart. Do you understand?"

Yvette nodded.

"Good. Now, how about a Britney Spears song?" Juliet started restacking the boxes. "She's my sister's favorite."

"Now do you believe me that Juliet's gone?" Jacqueline demanded after they'd scoured the gardens and found no sign of her.

Luc was trying to stay calm. "The junior gardener said he saw Juliet heading toward the head gardener's cottage early this morning."

"I know that. I was standing right beside you when he told you. But there's no one at the cottage now. We've been standing here pounding on the door for ages. And you even climbed in the open window to check things out and saw nothing suspicious. Right?"

"Right." No sign of forced entrance or of anything amiss. Spotting a child at the cottage next door, Luc motioned the boy over. He seemed more interested in Jacqueline's navel jewelry than Luc's questions. "Do you know Juliet Beaudreau?" Luc's voice was sharp.

The boy, who looked to be about nine or ten, nodded and swallowed nervously. "Have you seen her today?" Luc asked.

The boy nodded again.

"Do you know where she is?"

"A man came and took them away." The boy's voice quivered. "He took the gardener's wife and Julie."

"What man?"

"Henri, the footman."

"Celeste's favorite footman," Jacqueline declared. "Come on, let's go find him."

"You go stay with your grandmother. I'll deal with Henri alone."

"He's probably already left the palace," she warned him. "If he has, go find Celeste."

Luc was about to inform Jacqueline that he didn't need a twelve-year-old with purple hair telling him how to run an investigation, when he saw the fear in her eyes—eyes so similar to Juliet's. "Don't worry, Muffin. I'll find her." He gave her a brief hug.

"You'd better, Spyman." Her voice was jaunty but her smile was shaky. "Juliet is one of a kind. We can't lose her."

Luc deposited Jacqueline in the dowager queen's safe care before calling Alistair, the palace steward, on the palace phone. As Jacqueline had suspected, Henri had gone missing as well. Luc wasted no time, going directly to Queen Celeste's quarters.

He pounded on the door once before opening it.

"How dare you enter my quarters without my permission!" Celeste stood before him, dressed in an expensive designer suit and dripping in priceless jewels, the epitome of royal outrage. "Who do you think you are?"

"I'm the King of St. Michel and I want to know what you've done with Juliet."

"You're not the king yet." Her smile was more smirk than anything else.

"Is that a threat? Threatening the monarch is an offense punishable by life imprisonment, Celeste. I don't think you want to spend the rest of your days in a prison, now do you?"

Her confidence waned as the hard edge of his voice finally got through to her. "I don't know what you're talking about. I didn't threaten you. I'm a mere woman, still weak from birthing the king's child.''

"You haven't had a weak moment in your life."

She actually preened at his comment. She placed a conciliatory hand on his arm. "Perhaps we should work together, Luc. To unite St. Michel. If you were to marry me, then the people would be sure to accept you as their leader.''

He stepped away from her in disdain. "I wouldn't marry you if you were the last woman in the universe. So you can stop batting your eyes at me and keep your hands to yourself. I'm not buying the *femme fatale* routine."

For the first time, Celeste looked at him with a hint of fear. Good. He had his war face on, the one he used with terrorists and hardened criminals, the one that warned them that he'd just as soon stomp on them as talk to them. His voice turned as deadly as his expression. "You have ten seconds to tell me what you've done with Juliet. And if you've hurt her, I swear you'll pay with your life."

Celeste backed away from him, her eyes wide. "It wasn't my idea," she shrieked. "It was all Claude's fault."

"Claude?"

"Claude Guignard. He panicked, and he took Juliet."

"Took her where?" Luc loomed over Celeste as she sank back onto the ivory-and-gold pillows of her lush sofa.

"I don't know."

"I'm not buying that. Your ten seconds is just about

up," he growled. "Don't make me force you into telling me what you know."

"The warehouse," Celeste babbled, her upper lip dotted with sweat. "He took her to an abandoned warehouse...by the river...you'll find her locked up there."

"You'd better pray that I do find her and that she's unharmed. You'd better pray real hard, Celeste."

Luc left her cowering on the couch.

A second after he closed the doors, he heard her furious curses followed by the sound of something—a vase perhaps—smashing against the wall. "Don't let anyone in or out," he ordered the two guards he'd posted at either side of the entrance. "Under any circumstances."

Chapter Eleven

Luc heard Juliet before he saw her. He heard her singing a Sting song. At the top of her lungs.

He and the rest of his security force broke down the locked door into the warehouse as well as the one in the storage room. And then he had her safe in his arms.

She insisted on trying to tell him something about Celeste's baby, but he didn't care. All he cared about was Juliet.

He cupped her dusty face with his hands. "Are you all right? Did he hurt you?"

"I'm fine. I'm so glad you're here." She touched his cheek as if to confirm he was indeed real.

Luc took her into his arms again, kissing every inch of her face.

"Luc, I'm trying to tell you something important. Celeste switched babies with Yvette. Her child is actually a girl. This girl." She pointed to the baby in the bassinet.

"She screams almost as loudly as Celeste," he noted ruefully.

Juliet laughed unsteadily. ''Her diaper needs changing. The baby, I mean. Not Celeste. I'm babbling again, aren't I? I knew you'd come, I kept telling myself you'd come. I'm so thirsty.''

Luc quickly handed her a chilled bottle of water even as he nodded to his security officers to assist Yvette and her baby.

''Let's get you out of here and back to the palace.'' Luc kept his arm around Juliet as he guided her to his waiting car, complete with a driver.

''Did you hear what I said about Celeste swapping babies?'' Juliet asked as the sedan sped through the streets to the palace, led by a police escort that cleared the way through busy late-afternoon traffic.

''Yes, I heard.'' In the back seat of the large sedan, Luc tucked Juliet's head onto his shoulder and rested his chin atop her head, his arm remaining firmly around her as if he were afraid she might disappear at any moment.

''I promised Yvette you'd get her baby boy back for her.''

''I will.'' He ran his fingers through her hair, smoothing it out.

''You don't seem surprised by the news.''

''Nothing Celeste does surprises me any longer.''

''So now you believe me? I told you she was up to something.''

''Aside from swapping babies, she also conspired with Berg Dekker to overthrow the governments of Rhineland and St. Michel.''

''Oh, my.'' Juliet blinked in surprise. ''She has been busy. Where is she now?''

''Under house arrest at the palace.''

''So it's over?''

Touching her chin, he gently lifted her face to his. "One chapter is over, but the next is just beginning."

Thinking about the future made her stomach do somersaults in an unpleasant way. Juliet nervously swallowed a lump in her throat. "The dowager queen told me that the Privy Council would be meeting soon to declare you the king. I imagine that will be done even faster now."

Luc nodded, his expression growing more solemn. He might have said more, but they had arrived at the palace and his attention was required as he was bombarded with questions and demands from the prime minister the moment they stepped out of the sedan.

Juliet and Luc were separated by the crowd of servants and government workers who'd gathered to welcome them back to the palace. "Juliet!" Luc shouted.

"She's being taken care of by the dowager queen," the prime minister assured him, urgently tugging on his arm. "No need to concern yourself, your majesty. There's much to be done if we are to make the announcement of your impending coronation to the people of St. Michel in the morning."

Your majesty. The prime minister had just called him your majesty. For the first time it really sank in. This was it. No more time for adjusting. No more dress rehearsals or protocol lessons. This was it.

"Are you ready for the gala ball this evening?" the dowager queen asked as they took tea together in the White Drawing Room two days later.

"Yes, ma'am," Juliet dutifully replied, lying through her teeth.

"I told you to call me Simone. Or Grandmama, as Jacqueline does."

"Yes, ma'am, Grandmama." Flustered, Juliet set her

teacup down before she dropped it. Her fingers trembled. Nothing about her life seemed real anymore. She hadn't seen Luc since the prime minister had whisked him away almost forty-eight hours ago. Not in person, anyway. She'd seen him on the television as he'd addressed the nation. The dowager queen had been at his side, as had the three princesses. But not Juliet. Once again she was the outsider.

"She's nervous about the party tonight," her sister declared. The purple dye had washed out and left Jacqueline's hair its usual dark-blond color.

The dowager queen appeared surprised by this revelation. "Why should you be nervous, Juliet? You've attended royal functions before."

"Tonight is different," she replied.

"She wants to look her best for Luc."

"Jacqueline!" Juliet was tempted to throw the tray of scones at her sister. But then her emotions had been on edge ever since she'd been parted from Luc.

As promised, he'd reunited Yvette with her infant son. Yvette had stopped by to tell her the news, along with the information that Celeste had climbed down a drainpipe outside her apartment window and had escaped from the palace along with her lover Claude.

The baby girl that Celeste had actually given birth to was in the safekeeping of a nanny at the palace while DNA testing was done to confirm the little one's paternity. Should Claude turn out to be the biological father, then Yvette had offered to raise the baby along with her own son. Otherwise, if she truly was King Philippe's daughter, Luc had vowed to take care of the little girl.

Juliet could understand that with all that going on, he'd had his hands full. But he could have called her, written her an e-mail, something. He was in the same palace, having moved into the king's apartments. If it weren't for the servants, she wouldn't know anything. What did it say about her that she felt closer to them than to the royal family?

"Daydreaming about Luc?" Jacqueline teased her.

Juliet's fingers itched to reach for the scones and toss a few in Jacqueline's direction, but she valiantly restrained herself once again. "No, I was thinking about the festivities this evening. It's been a while since we've ever had such a grand party. Queen Regina once had a garden party and invited every citizen of St. Michel to come. I believe four thousand attended that event."

"Well, we haven't gone quite that far, but everyone who's anyone will be there tonight. Not just the aristocracy, but the business and education leaders as well." The dowager queen took a sip of tea. "The event is meant to introduce the country to their new king. As you know, the coronation will take place at the end of the week."

"Two days from now. I had no idea you'd be able to arrange everything that quickly."

"We've had the procedure in place for hundreds of years. And we've been waiting since my son's passing to crown the next king. It promises to be a joyous occasion."

"So, Juliet, are you wearing that revealing Versace gown like the one Jennifer Lopez wore to the Grammy Awards?" Jacqueline's eyes gleamed with devilish humor.

"No, *I'm* going to wear that gown," the dowager queen replied, without batting an eye.

Juliet and Jacqueline both burst into laughter—Jacqueline with delight, Juliet with guilty pleasure. Putting her hand to her lips, Juliet eyed the older woman uncertainly before relaxing upon seeing the dowager queen's smile.

"And I'm sure you'll look lovely in it…Grandmama," Juliet said.

"Thank you, Juliet. And what about you? What are you wearing this evening?"

"Something that covers her from head to toe probably," Jacqueline replied on her behalf.

"Since the infamous Versace gown is already taken—" Juliet shared a grin with the dowager queen "—I guess I'll have to make do with something else."

"Something else that covers her from head to toe." Jacqueline's voice was gloomy as she reached for another tea cake, this one shaped like a flower.

"You don't have to make do with anything," the dowager queen told Juliet. With a tilt of her regal head she motioned to the footman on duty, who opened the doors and ushered in a chic-looking woman dressed in a gorgeous suit the shade of periwinkle. "This is Madame Chantille, the most talented dress designer in all of Europe."

"You are too kind, your highness."

"And these are my granddaughters. Do you think you can fix them up a bit for tonight's party?"

Madame Chantille studied them for a moment before nodding emphatically. "Leave them in my capable hands, ma'am, and I'll transform them into the belles of the ball."

Luc tried not to sigh impatiently as his valet slipped on his jacket for him. He'd been putting on his own jacket for more than twenty years, but now that he was a king he was no longer allowed that luxury.

The royal attire featured the deep blue and red of St.

Michel's national colors. The military-style jacket was filled with medals along the right breast pocket, each one indicating some special point in the country's history. Luc hadn't had time to learn the names of all the medals yet, he'd been too busy trying to memorize his lines for the coronation on Sunday.

The Privy Council had performed a private ceremony with only themselves present so that Luc could assume his duties immediately. And what a mountain of paperwork had awaited him! He'd had nonstop meetings with the cabinet members of the government and had hardly slept since returning to the palace, but what irked him most was that he had yet to see Juliet.

He'd sent her a corsage for tonight and told her to save him the first dance. He'd also assigned a guard to watch her, wanting to make sure she was safe even though Celeste and Claude had fled the continent and were on their way to South America, to a country without an extradition agreement with St. Michel. He did take some pleasure in knowing that the royal jewels she'd taken with her were fakes, replaced by the dowager queen when her son had first announced his engagement to Celeste.

It was easier for Luc to think of King Philippe as the dowager queen's son than as his own father. In his heart of hearts, Albert would always be his father. Albert had sent his regrets that he couldn't attend the festivities tonight, but said he'd be there for the coronation ceremony on Sunday.

The promise of seeing Juliet tonight was the one thing that had kept Luc going. His valet placed the rich red satin royal banner across Luc's chest and pinned it in place with the Cross of St. Michel. Luc looked in the mirror…and saw a king.

Twenty minutes later Luc looked across the crowded Crystal Ballroom…and saw Juliet.

Juliet had never seen the Crystal Ballroom look lovelier. Except perhaps for that night when she'd attempted to give Luc dancing lessons, when he'd lit candles and played Strauss waltzes on a boom box. The first time he kissed her. Tonight a string quartet provided the music and the priceless Austrian crystal chandeliers were all lit up, showering the room with mini-rainbows dancing off the numerous tiers of faceted crystals.

The mirrored walls reflected the beautiful people in their gorgeous gowns and elegant tuxedos. Footmen, attired in their most formal livery of red jackets and pants, were stationed around the perimeter of the huge ballroom, ready with silver trays of slender Bohemian crystal fluted glasses filled with St. Michel's best champagne.

Juliet also caught sight of the three de Bergeron sisters. The romantic Marie-Claire was with her aristocratic businessman husband Sebastian, who could give George Clooney a run for his money. At one point in the search for the missing heir, Sebastian's manipulative mother had claimed that he was Katie's child. Juliet could only imagine how upset that must have made Marie-Claire, who was already half in love with him. The truth had come out, and Sebastian had gone on to marry Marie-Claire in a lovely ceremony.

Ariane, the middle sister, was laughing at something her husband Prince Etienne of Rhineland had just said to her.

The eldest princess, Lise, was gazing up adoringly at her new husband Charles Rodin. Lise, several months pregnant, had that wonderful glow about her. Juliet had never seen her look happier.

All three woman looked stunning with their blond hair and light eyes. Juliet was certain that the dowager queen didn't have to call in a specialist to help any of them. They all knew what to wear, how to look gorgeous naturally. It had taken a team of five to make Juliet look this good.

But she did look good. Even she was willing to acknowledge that much. In fact, she looked almost beautiful.

Catching a glimpse of her reflection in the mirrored walls, she almost didn't recognize herself. Madame Chantille had chosen a magically divine dress in white and silver that shimmered with every step Juliet took. The strapless top hugged her body, showing off her bare shoulders, while the rich drape of the material added grace to her appearance by its sheer elegance as it curved in at her waist before flaring out in a full-length skirt. Her hair, behaving perfectly for once, was arranged in a cascade of curls falling from the top of her head.

She hoped Luc recognized her. She had yet to catch sight of him.

The ceiling-to-floor French doors were open to the large terrace leading down to the gardens, allowing the fragrance of old-fashioned roses to perfume the room. Juliet paused to smile and chat with one of the footmen who'd recently become engaged.

Her sister tugged on her arm. "Did you see Luc? Talk about a hottie!"

Juliet didn't even bother reprimanding her sister. "Where is he?"

"On his way over here. Ten people have stopped him to talk with him, so it's taking him a while, but he's almost here. Hey, Spyman, how's it going?"

Luc smiled. "I haven't spilled anything yet, Muffin,

so I'd say it's going okay. Better now that your sister is here. You look breathtaking, Juliet.''

She shyly lifted her gaze to his. "Thank you.''

His vivid blue eyes searched her face, then wandered over her body in a visual tour that was as seductive as a touch. The surrounding crowd seemed to fade into the background as Juliet's entire focus was fixed on him.

He looked incredibly good in the formal attire of the King of St. Michel. Still, she'd always have a special affection for him wearing his biker black jeans and black T-shirt. And then there was his classy sophistication in a tuxedo. Tonight he had a regal bearing that suited him well but made her very aware of his newfound position.

"I see you're wearing the corsage I sent you.'' His voice was husky.

"Yes.''

"You two are just a fountain of dazzling conversation,'' Jacqueline mocked them both. "I'm off to find a drink. A soft drink, so you can relax, big sister. Did you know she could look this good, Spyman?''

"She always looks good to me,'' Luc replied.

His smile made Juliet feel like Cinderella at the ball. But she didn't have long to bask in the moment before the prime minister interrupted them.

"There you are, your majesty. It's time for you to speak to the crowd. Actually, we're already ten minutes behind schedule.'' With his pewter-grey hair and mustache, the normally dignified statesman appeared a tad agitated. "We can't delay any longer.''

"Wait for me,'' Luc told Juliet. "I'll be back.''

As the two men made their way to the decorated dais at the corner of the ballroom, Juliet heard the comments from the women around her—comments about Luc's good looks and his being proclaimed Europe's most eligible bachelor in the tabloids that morning.

As the crowd moved forward to hear Luc's official statement welcoming everyone to the palace tonight, Juliet chose to stay by the cooling breeze wafting in through the open French doors. She was admiring how well Luc held himself, how confidently he spoke to the huge crowd, when a man's voice from her past interrupted her.

"Still spending your time daydreaming, Juliet?"

"Armand!" Her stomach dropped as she turned to face him. "What are you doing here?"

"I'm an invited guest, just as you are."

Clearly his way of making her feel like an outsider in the palace. Looking at him now she was astonished that she'd ever thought him good-looking. Not that he'd changed that much. But she had.

She was older and wiser now. She could see the lines of weakness in his tanned face, the meanness beneath his surface smile, the self-absorption of his entire attitude. He had light-brown hair perfectly cut and a square jaw that suited a male model. But there was no one inside the pretty outer shell.

Luc had more sex appeal in his little finger than Armand could ever have. She'd been lucky to have discovered Armand for the shallow man he was before it had been too late.

That didn't mean she wanted to have a conversation with him now, or at any other time for that matter.

"Nice dress," Armand casually noted. "Someone must have helped you pick it out. I always told you that you needed an image consultant."

Bull's-eye. A direct hit on her self-confidence. And he said it with such charm, too.

Keeping his eyes on Luc, Armand said, "Quite a story,

the missing heir turning out to be right under our noses all this time. The press is having a field day with it all. In order to restore credibility to the throne our new king will need a *real* royal to show him the ropes. There are a number of European princesses who could be excellent candidates. Already tonight, Wilmena of Saxony has made some inroads, but the young princess from Liechtenstein may well give her a run for her money. Some of my associates tell me that they've already started a betting pool regarding the identity of our future queen. So far Wilmena is the odds-on favorite. She comes from an old and prestigious family."

The more Armand talked, the more inadequate Juliet felt. She had to get away from him. "Excuse me, but I must go check on my sister."

"Oh, your *half* sister, you mean. Don't let me keep you." Armand's smile was a double-edged sword that cut even further into her dwindling confidence. It was as if he knew that it had taken a team to make her look like Cinderella at the ball, and that at midnight she'd return to what she always had been—the nondescript dark-haired woman lost amid her beautiful blond sisters.

Juliet walked away, but knew she needed a break entirely from the ballroom, so she slipped out the next set of French doors to the terrace, down the wide steps to the gardens that had always given her peace. She'd no sooner settled on a bench then she was joined by someone.

"Ah, Mademoiselle Beaudreau, just the person I was searching for." The proclamation came from none other than the head of the Privy Council, Baron Severin.

Juliet knew the history of the Privy Council, about the combination of ancient European aristocratic titles—one earl, one duke, one count and one baron.

Baron Severin was the only person who scored higher on the intimidation scale than the dowager queen. He possessed the upright bearing of a military man and had a thick head of white hair. While not wearing his ceremonial robes this evening, he still looked as powerful as he was.

She couldn't imagine why he'd be looking for her, but she didn't think it could be a good sign. Unless he had some sort of historical question about the coronation on Sunday?

She tried to think positively.

"I won't beat about the bush, young lady. I saw you frolicking in the fountain with young Luc. That kind of unsuitable behavior is not befitting our new King Luc. Things are different now. More is expected of him. His every move will be closely monitored, by the press and by the people of St. Michel. While that kind of common behavior may be acceptable for you, it is not for him. We must be certain that his past mistakes aren't repeated. His associates have to be of the highest calibre. Surely you understand what I'm saying?"

She nodded. Baron Severin was saying she was a mistake, a bad influence on Luc. She sat motionless, caught in the grip of an anguish too deep to manage.

"He'll be expected to make a royal marriage, uniting the de Bergeron family name with one of equal stature from within the aristocracy of Europe."

"I understand," she whispered.

"I thought you might. An intelligent girl like yourself had to realize the damage you were doing."

His words were like poisoned arrows piercing her soul. Armand's earlier comments had opened the lid on her self-doubts, but the baron had just put the nail in the coffin, killing any hope she might have.

Everything he'd said was true. Unlike Armand, the baron wasn't trying to hurt her, wasn't trying to make trouble. He was simply pointing out the facts.

She'd become a liability to Luc. There was only one thing to do. Leave. Immediately.

Chapter Twelve

Inside her private rooms, Juliet didn't bother changing clothes. Instead she tossed a few things into a bag, her hands quivering as she grabbed her belongings without any sense of order. She stopped as she reached for the black sundress she'd worn when Luc had taken her to the carnival.

Remembering that night made her crumple onto the bed, silent tears pouring down her cheeks. As her pain increased, so did the need to get away. She left the rest of her things behind, including that dress. She could always have some things shipped to her later. When she decided where she was going.

She hastily scribbled a disjointed note to Jacqueline saying she needed to get away and apologizing for missing the new king's coronation. She was sure they'd all get along without her.

Including Luc.

She knew Luc had feelings for her—feelings of friendship, perhaps even more than that. But because she loved him so much, she couldn't be the one to bring dishonor upon him. He had a path very different from hers.

She had to set him free. And she had to do it now, this very moment, while she still had the courage, while the baron's words still burned in her soul.

If she saw Luc again, she'd weaken. She couldn't say goodbye, couldn't even leave a note for him. She had to cut it off entirely. It was best this way.

Her heart was breaking, but she was doing the right thing. That knowledge should have made her feel better, lessened her anguish in some small way. But it didn't.

Grabbing her belongings, she hurried down the deserted marble hallways. The joyous sounds of music and people laughing drifted up from the ballroom, mocking her as she made her silent escape. She raced out a side entrance of the palace, past a startled Alistair. Her compact car was just as she'd left it, parked outside the royal garages, unfit to rub bumpers with the exclusive Mercedes and BMWs inside.

It only took her a moment to stow her things. As she gathered the skirts of her dress and slid behind the steering wheel, she vowed that she'd return the dress to the dowager queen the next day, sending it by insured shipper. She needed to start making a list of things she had to do.

Staying focused on that prevented her from crying. The insides of her eyelids felt like gritty sandpaper from keeping the tears at bay. But that was a good thing, because it meant her vision wasn't blurred, and she could drive away from the palace without further delay. She refused to even allow herself one final look in her rearview mirror.

She had to be strong. She'd known this moment was coming. She'd always known she hadn't quite fitted in.

Close, but not close enough. Always an "almost." Never good enough. There was no changing that.

She'd been foolish to think otherwise. Fairy tales didn't come true for girls like her. The privileged and gorgeous de Bergeron daughters—they were the heroines in the classic tales, the ones who got their happy endings.

Juliet should have stuck to her books. That was the world she belonged in, the quiet peaceful world of history and academic work. Maybe she'd become a professor of history.

She should add that to her list. Right after Find a place to live away from St. Michel, and Return ballgown to the dowager queen. She doubted the older woman would want her calling her Grandmama any longer.

"You did a wonderful job with your welcome speech, Luc," his grandmother, the dowager queen, congratulated him.

"Thank you." His attention quickly wandered over the crowd. "Have you seen Juliet? I asked her to wait here for me."

"Already ordering the girl about, are you?"

He smiled a bit sheepishly. "She's accused me of being bossy in the past."

"She's a good girl."

"She's more than that." Luc wasn't certain when the first realization had come that he loved her. That night he'd kissed her in this very ballroom? The night he'd whisked her off to the carnival? When he'd almost made love to her? Or when he'd almost lost her to Celeste's evil plot?

The awareness of his emotions hadn't struck him like a thunderbolt out of the blue. Instead it had crept up on him like a gentle breeze, infiltrating his very soul until he knew that his life lacked all meaning without Juliet. It might seem as if one day she'd been just a friend and the next she was indispensable to him, but in the past few weeks his feelings for her had been undergoing a powerful transformation.

"So you have special feelings for her?" his grand-mother asked. "Beyond friendship?"

Luc nodded.

She gave him one of her laser stares. "And your intentions toward her are honorable?"

"Yes. But I don't know that she'll want me. I'm no prize."

"You're a king!"

"A definite handicap in her book," Luc noted dryly. "Juliet has no desire for life in the limelight. And if she marries me, she will be thrust into the spotlight."

His grandmother placed a reassuring hand on his arm. "Juliet is stronger than you give her credit for."

"I know she's strong. I also know that none of this—" He waved his hand at the surrounding crowd "—is her idea of a good time. She'd much rather be reading a good book."

"She'd much rather be in your arms," his grandmother said with a sparkle in her eyes. "Go on, go find her and tell her how you feel. Life is too short to wait, you need to grab your happiness and follow your heart. I'll support you, Luc. I won't make the same mistake I made with my son, I promise you that."

"Thank you, Grandmother." He kissed her cheek. "You have a heart of gold after all."

"Just be sure you don't let anyone else know about that. I have a reputation to uphold, you know." She playfully smacked his hand with the painted fan she'd used to cool herself with all evening. "Now be off with you!"

* * *

Juliet had brought the kittens with her in a cat carrier placed on the floor of the passenger seat. Their mews made her feel guilty for taking them, but she'd needed them. She was leaving everything else she loved behind. Surely she could be forgiven for taking Mittens and Rascal?

Tears threatened again but she bit her lip to keep them away. There was no time for weakness now. She'd think about everything later, when she was safely away. At the moment she was heading toward France, and she'd stop whenever she got tired. She'd always wanted to take a road trip, have the freedom to come and go as she pleased. This was her chance.

She turned on the car radio, not too loud so as not to scare the kittens, but when Sting's song "Brand New Day" came on, she had to turn it off again. Luc liked Sting's music. Too many memories there.

She'd driven several kilometers from the palace when she heard the sound of a police siren. Glancing at the speedometer, she muttered under her breath as she realized she'd been going over the posted speed limit. Sure enough, the police car pulled her over to the side of the road.

Sighing, she turned and reached into her purse for her license. "I'm sorry. I know I was going a bit too fast," she began apologizing when she looked up at the official standing at her car door. It wasn't any ordinary St. Michel police officer.

It was Luc. Still wearing his royal uniform.

She was stunned. "What are you doing here? How did you know where to find me? How did you even know I'd left?"

"My grandmother saw you driving out. I had a secu-

rity car trail you until I could get here and take charge
of things myself. You are in serous trouble. You've been
accused of stealing the King of St. Michel's heart." His
voice and expression were stern, but his eyes—his eyes
positively ate her up. "Do you have anything to say in
your own defense?"

"Yes." No matter how he looked at her, she had to
be strong. "I'm not the kind of queen you need."

"You're the *woman* I need," Luc fiercely interrupted
her, yanking open the car door and tugging her into his
arms. "You're the woman I *love*. I'm nothing without
you."

She blinked her tears away. "You're the King of St.
Michel."

"I'm Luc and I love you. Marry me. Help me. Laugh
with me. Love me."

"Oh Luc, I already do love you! That's why I had to
leave. Don't you see?"

"All I see is you."

"That's the problem then. You're too close to me to
see the situation objectively. Baron Severin isn't."

Luc frowned. "What does he have to do with anything?"

"He talked to me tonight, pointed out some things that
I already knew."

"Like what?"

"Like the fact that you need someone of royal blood,
as you are."

Luc swore under his breath. "The baron is dead
wrong. The dowager queen has already given us her
blessing."

"The baron told me that I was hurting you by frolicking in the fountain with you," she countered unsteadily.

"The only thing that could hurt me is your leaving

me.'' She could see his pain in the clenching of his jaw, in the stormy anguish reflected deep in his blue eyes. ''Promise me you'll never do it again. Promise you'll marry me.''

''Luc, you haven't thought this through—''

''Of course I have.'' He tilted his head at her, lifting one dark eyebrow in that way she loved. ''I always think things through, you know that about me.''

''I thought you didn't believe in love, that it made a man vulnerable.''

''It's certainly made me vulnerable.'' He placed her open palm on his chest right over his heart. He stared down at her, his compelling blue eyes smoldering with passion, desire and most important…love. ''Do you feel that? My heart is beating for you. If being king means I can't have you, then I'll refuse the position, call off the coronation.''

''You can't do that!''

''I certainly can. And I will if you don't marry me. Because I'm not ruling as king without you by my side as my queen.'' His voice was suspiciously hoarse, making him sound like a man at the end of his emotional rope.

''Oh, Luc.'' She lifted her hand to his face and stood on tiptoe to place a tender string of kisses across his beloved face. ''I love you so much. I was just trying to do the right thing.''

''The right thing is marrying me. Will you be my wife?''

Here it was. That fork in the road of her future. Which should she take—the safe path that kept her life quiet or the risky one that kept her with Luc? In the end, the decision was inevitable. Knowing he loved her was the missing key. She couldn't leave him. ''Yes. Yes, I will.''

"Thank God." Luc lowered his mouth to hers for a kiss of dedicated passion and lifelong commitment.

"We'll just add a wedding ceremony to the coronation," he murmured against her lips as he trailed kisses across her face. "Everybody is already gathered together, we might as well kill two birds with one stone.

"Kill two birds, hmm? How romantic," she teased him with a laugh. "Is this what I have to look forward to for the next fifty years together?"

"The next *seventy* years, and I'll show you what you have to look forward to." He kissed her again, this time incorporating all their joy and laughter.

A short while later, they transferred her belongings and the kittens into the back of the police car he'd commandeered, leaving her car by the side of the road for a member of the security force to drive back. On their way to the palace, Juliet voiced her concerns. "Are you sure about this? A wedding in two days?"

"I'm positive." Luc flashed her a smile of utter confidence. "How difficult can it be?"

"You want to do *what?*" his grandmother practically shrieked as she sat in the White Drawing Room and stared at Luc and Juliet in disbelief.

"You heard me. I want to marry Juliet right before the coronation. You told me you approved," Luc reminded her.

"Of marrying her, yes. Of doing it on Sunday, no. I never said that was a good idea."

"Perhaps we should wait," Juliet said hesitantly.

"I'm not going to be crowned king without her," he said curtly, with a warning look at his grandmother.

She met his gaze head-on and impatiently tapped her

foot on the floor for good measure. "Luc, you're bullying the girl. Have you asked Juliet what she wants to do?"

"He's not really bullying me, ma'am," Juliet earnestly assured the dowager queen. "I wouldn't let him get away with bullying me. He's just being his regular bossy self."

"I told you to call me Grandmama." She smiled at Juliet. "Now, what made you take off from the ball this evening?"

Luc answered on Juliet's behalf. "That old windbag Baron Severin came after her tonight and fed her a load of garbage about her not being fit because she's not royalty. I want the man banished from the country."

Juliet had to laugh.

"What?" Luc turned to frown at her. "The man insulted you. He made you run away from me. He's lucky I don't toss him into the dungeon."

"He didn't insult me, he was just concerned about my suitability to be your wife. And he didn't make me do anything. It was my own insecurities that made me leave. But that was before I knew you loved me." She squeezed his hand, which had been clasping hers since they'd arrived at the palace. "Now nothing could make me leave your side."

"Not even the entire Privy Council throwing a hissy fit?"

She grinned at him. "Not even that."

"I told you she was a good girl," his grandmother said rather proudly. "Now, about setting a date for the wedding…"

"We're getting married on Sunday," Luc repeated.

"Is this agreeable to you, Juliet? It's your wedding day, too. Most brides want time to plan their special day."

"I've already got the dress," Juliet confessed.

"That slinky black one?" Luc asked hopefully.

The dowager queen's voice was horrified. "She is not getting married in black!"

"No, it's based on Queen Regina's wedding dress," Juliet quickly inserted. "A friend of mine in Paris made one up for me several years ago. She was a fashion design major and had to do a wedding dress…so I had her do this one. I always thought it was too lovely to actually wear."

"Do you have it here at the palace?"

Juliet nodded. "I was going to use it as part of my thesis presentation."

"I think you'll be putting it to a much better use this way," the dowager queen stated.

"I agree." Luc put his arm around Juliet and hugged her to his side.

His grandmother eyed them both doubtfully. "But still, we have less than forty-eight hours…."

"No wedding, no coronation," Luc stated.

His grandmother threw her hands in the air. "All right, all right. I didn't say it would be impossible. Just difficult."

Luc leaned down to kiss her. "You can manage 'difficult' with both hands tied behind your back."

"You charming sweet-talker, you. All right, leave it to me," his grandmother stated in her most regal voice. "We'll have your wedding on Sunday."

"I really don't need a bridal shower," Juliet was telling the dowager queen the next evening.

"Nonsense. It's tradition. My granddaughters have a lovely evening planned for you. Come, it's time to open your gifts. We all worked together on this."

"Before we start, there's something I've been meaning

to say." Ariane stood to face Juliet. "I know that throughout the years, while you never actually said anything about it, you've never quite felt as if you fit in, and I feel badly that I never did more to make you feel welcome."

"Me, too," Marie-Claire said.

"And I do, as well," Lise agreed.

Juliet blinked away the tears. "Thank you. That's so sweet of you all. I realize now that my feelings of insecurity were rooted within me and weren't caused by any of you deliberately trying to make me feel like an outsider."

"Maybe so, but we could have done more, included you more. We were too self-absorbed," Ariane said.

"We were princesses, it was our job to be self-absorbed." Marie-Claire grinned.

"Anyway, as Grandmama said, we all got together in planning our gifts for you," Jacqueline continued. "Not that you gave us much time, but we like a challenge, or so Grandmama tells us. Our theme, of course, is something old, something new, something borrowed, something blue."

"Open this one first." Ariane handed her a large box, beautifully wrapped.

Inside, Juliet found a gorgeous antique veil. "It's the veil I wore at my wedding," the dowager queen said.

"And I at mine," Marie-Claire said.

"Then I wore it at my wedding," Ariane said. "Now we would love for you to wear it."

Nothing could have indicated more their intention to include her as family, and nothing could have touched her more. For the first time in her life she really felt at home with these women. Juliet blinked, the tears in her eyes right on the verge of rolling down her cheeks. "I don't know what to say," she whispered, "except thank you so very much."

"I get to wear the veil after you," Jacqueline said. "As my something borrowed."

Juliet laughed. "I hope not for a few years yet."

The presents continued—a lovely string of pearls from Ariane for something new, a beautiful set of antique cameo earrings from Lise for something old, a racy pale-blue lingerie set from Marie-Claire, and, from the royal jewels, a stunning sapphire bracelet from the dowager queen as something blue. The bracelet matched the ring that she and Luc had selected from the many rings in the royal collection.

And from Jacqueline came a ring box. "It's not sapphires or anything like that," she warned, a bit self-consciously. "It's our mother's ring. With posies all around it. It's very small, but I thought you'd like to wear it as a pinkie ring when you get married. Do you like it?"

Juliet responded with a huge hug. Their mother hadn't had much jewelry, because when she'd married King Philippe, he'd insisted she give it all away and start fresh. This ring was the only thing she'd kept. "Thank you." Looking over her younger sister's head, she told everyone, "Thank you all!"

"Well, now." Juliet could almost have sworn she saw a shimmer of tears in the dowager queen's eyes as she announced, "It's after nine. I fear that Jacqueline and I will have to leave now. We need our beauty sleep."

"Me, too," Lise said. "A pregnant woman needs her rest."

"So do I," Juliet said. "After all, I'm getting married in the morning."

"No, you stay a little longer," the dowager queen told

her. "Ariane and Marie-Claire have something else for you."

Ariane waited until they'd left before turning to Juliet. "Given the premise that less is more, I've arranged for a little entertainment for us this evening."

"Did you get the Dauberville String Quartet?" Juliet inquired.

Ariane shook her head. "No, they weren't available. Alistair," she addressed the always reserved palace steward, "is the entertainment ready?"

Alistair fixed her with a disapproving look before donning his customary look of blandness. "Yes, your highness."

"Good. Tell them to proceed. Come sit down, Juliet. Right here on this couch. Yes, that should give you a good view."

View? Of what? A second later Juliet had her answer as the door to the Ruby Salon burst open and a quartet of men marched in.

"I told you to get good-looking men for this job," Marie-Claire hissed to her sister.

Ariane shrugged. "They were all booked. Regular Joe Party Boys Incorporated were all that was left at such short notice."

Juliet stared in disbelief at the out-of-shape, middle-aged men who were gyrating madly to the sound of "I'm Too Sexy." Then they ripped open their shirts, revealing bulging bellies. She felt like sinking under the couch.

Just when she thought matters couldn't get any worse, as the men finished their production number by prancing in thongs, revealing a row of pudgy behinds, Luc walked into the room.

Juliet sent him a silent plea to rescue her from this fiasco, but he just grinned at her. "Sorry to interrupt. I can see you ladies are busy at present. I'll come back a bit later.''

"No, Luc, wait!" Juliet called out, but he was gone.

Ten minutes later the exotic dancers, as they called themselves, had completed their act and departed. Ariane and Marie-Claire were still wiping tears of mirth from their eyes, and Juliet had had to giggle a time or two herself at the men's deliberately outrageous moves. They'd clearly been laughing at themselves and enjoying every moment of it.

"Now can I go to bed?" Juliet asked the sisters.

"Not quite yet," Alistair surprised everyone by saying. "There's one more item on the agenda this evening."

"Did you arrange this?" Ariane asked Marie-Claire, who shook her head.

The music this time was Carly Simon's classic "Simply the Best." Alistair stepped out of the room and the door opened. Juliet, Ariane and Marie-Claire all gasped simultaneously.

For in walked three sexy men dressed in flowing white shirts and well-fitted jeans. And they weren't just any three men—they were none other than Marie-Claire's husband Sebastian, Ariane's husband Prince Etienne, and Juliet's fiancé Luc.

Of course, Juliet only had eyes for Luc. "We heard you ladies were looking for a little entertainment this evening," he drawled, his smoky blue gaze fixed on Juliet.

A moment later, they ripped off their shirts and let them drop to the floor. Juliet's heart raced at the sight of Luc wearing nothing but a wicked grin and jeans that hung low on his lean hips, revealing his sexy navel.

Coming closer, Luc held out his hand, inviting her to join with him in a royal version of salsa dancing that was more like swaying to the music while wrapped in each other's arms, his thighs pressed between hers.

"Never let it be said the de Bergeron girls don't know how to throw a bridal shower!" Ariane and Marie-Claire laughed as they and their husbands danced their way out of the room.

"And never let it be said that their men don't know how to keep them on their toes and make them happy," Luc added with a wicked smile.

The only thing Juliet remembered about her wedding the next afternoon was Luc looking incredibly handsome as he said his vows to her. The Victorian-style wedding dress Juliet's friend had made looked wonderful with the dowager queen's veil and the jewelry her sisters had given her.

Juliet felt part of a strong bond as she smiled at the sisters, who were her bridesmaids—Jacqueline, Ariane, Marie-Claire and Lise. All were lovely in ivory gowns shimmering with beadwork. Once again, the dowager queen's favorite dressmaker Madame Chantille had come to the rescue. And Juliet's brother Georges had flown in from summer skiing in South America to give Juliet away.

It was a perfect day.

The coronation ceremony would begin immediately following their wedding. The body of the St. Michel Cathedral was packed. Invitations were at a premium and overflow accommodation was provided in the gallery above the east door. Some sixty European royals were there, filling the pews. Television cameras covered the ceremony while reporters waited outside.

But, just as last night, Juliet only had eyes for Luc. She said her vows with the utter confidence of a woman marrying the man she loved. And when the priest said, "You may now kiss your bride, your majesty," Luc lifted the veil from her face and took Juliet in his arms.

Her happiness was complete, not with this happy ending but with this happy beginning of the rest of her life—a life shared with Luc.

Epilogue

One year later...

Juliet sadly shook her head at King Luc of St. Michel. "I never thought you'd leave me for another woman."

"I didn't leave you," Luc denied as he climbed back into bed with her. "I just went to change Michelle's diaper."

Juliet sighed. "She's a gorgeous baby girl, isn't she? And I'm not just saying that because she's my daughter."

"Of course not."

She gazed at him earnestly. "I mean, other babies are cute. Yvette's two little ones, Anise and Paul, are cute." DNA testing had confirmed that Celeste's baby girl had indeed been sired by her lover Claude and not by King Philippe. Yvette had renamed her son Paul and, as promised, was raising both children as her own with assistance from the palace. Luc had said, rightly so, that it wasn't fair to burden Yvette with the extra cost of another child without providing financial help.

"Yes, they are cute and a handful now that they are over a year old."

"And Lise's little girl is adorable, as is Ariane's newborn son. And Marie-Claire told me just yesterday that she's pregnant."

"First you girls all get married within a few months, now you all have babies." He shook his head.

"We're a close family," Juliet noted with a grin. "But our Michelle is special."

"Of course she is. I'm sure she smiled at me while I changed her diaper tonight."

"She probably was showing her appreciation, not only for the changing of her diaper but for the changing of the constitution, allowing females to inherit the throne of St. Michel."

Luc shrugged modestly. "It was nothing. It was time for St. Michel to join the twenty-first century."

"It was a big thing, Luc."

"Want me to show you another big thing?" he murmured seductively, snaring her in his arms.

"Why, you wicked man, you!" She pulled him even closer.

"I was referring to my smile. What did you think I meant?"

Juliet just grinned at him. "I love you so much, Luc."

"Show me," he whispered.

She did, with great enthusiasm. She'd found her prince at last and he was the king of her heart.

* * * * *

Look for Cathie Linz's next
MEN OF HONOR *title,*
MARRIED TO A MARINE,
in September 2002,
only from Silhouette Romance.

Do you want more Royally Wed *titles?*
Visit www.eHarlequin.com to find
more stories in this theme
and to read our free short story
THE PRINCE'S PROPOSAL
by Carla Cassidy.
Turn the page
for a glimpse into this world....

Chapter One

"I gave you a year to find a bride." King Michael Stanbury of Edenbourg glared at his one and only son, Nicholas. "In three weeks time that year will be up and you are no closer to marrying."

"I haven't found anyone appropriate yet," Nicholas replied.

"Nonsense. You have dated women from all over the world, any one of which would have made a fine wife."

Nicholas sighed. He couldn't very well tell his father that although the women he dated were beautiful, sophisticated and charming, he'd been looking for something more. "I thought it might be interesting if I married a woman I loved."

Michael snorted with displeasure. "Love is overrated. If you are to one day be king, you can't wait around for sentimental foolishness. If I'd had my way, I would have chosen a woman for you a long time ago, but your mother indulges you and insisted I give you time to find your own wife."

Nicholas bit back an angry retort. When his father had told him he had a year to marry, it hadn't sounded like an indulgence, it had been a royal dictate—as had most of his father's words to him over the years.

And as usual, Nicholas's first instinct was to rebel. He drew a deep breath. "Father, I have tried—"

"Not enough," King Michael said. "A wife gives a man an aura of stability and if you are not married by your 30th birthday, then I will not allow you to succeed the throne."

Nicholas wanted to protest the three-week deadline, tell his father it was a ridiculous ultimatum, but he knew it was useless.

King Michael rose from his chair and looked at his watch. "You'd better get dressed—the ball starts in an hour. Royalty from a dozen countries will be in attendance, surely you can find a woman that will make an appropriate princess."

Without another word, the king swept out of the room. As always, after a talk with his father, frustration gnawed at Nicholas.

He knew his father was right. It was time…past time that he chose a wife. He picked up his dress jacket and ran his thumb across the embroidered family crest on the lapel.

Besides, he'd spent the past year searching for love and had found it elusive. His father was right. Love was nothing more than sentimental foolishness. It was time to put aside such foolishness. It was time to do his duty. Time to choose a wife.

He knew the moment he saw her that she was the one. Prince Nicholas watched the dark-haired beauty from across the room. She stood by his cousin, Princess Serena of Wynborough, and Serena's husband, Gabriel Morgan.

He moved across the polished dance floor toward her. As he approached, she threw back her head and laughed at something Gabriel said and in her smile, in her rich laughter, Nicholas made up his mind.

He stopped in front of the woman, bowed, and held out a hand. "May I have this dance?"

Her brown eyes widened slightly as she nodded and smiled.

"Are you enjoying your visit to Wynborough?" he asked, noting that she smelled as sweet as she looked.

"Very much, although I'm finding things quite different here from my home in Brookville, Iowa." Again she offered him a shy smile. "I know you're the Prince of Edenbourg, but I'm afraid I'm not exactly sure where Edenbourg is."

Nicholas smiled, finding her confession charming.

"A long way from Wynborough. Edenbourg is in Eastern Europe."

"Have you visited here often? I understand you're Serena's first cousin."

"Actually, this is my first visit. Our families have not been close, although I enjoyed a long lunch with Serena yesterday." And throughout that lunch, Serena had spoken quite highly of her husband's relative, Rebecca Baxter. Now Nicholas tried to remember what his cousin had said about the lovely woman he held in his arms.

They spoke no more through the course of the dance. Nicholas's father's words rang in his ears. Time to find a bride. And why not the woman in his arms? Rebecca appealed to him more than any of the women he'd dated over the past year. That she was an American, and a commoner to boot, would irritate his father, but that only made her more desirable as far as Nicholas was concerned. Lust at first sight might make the best reason for marriage after all.

When the dance ended, Nicholas escorted her over to where his father stood. The king raised an eyebrow and Nicholas nodded.

So there would be no mistaking his intentions, he acted on an ancient custom. Reaching out to a nearby floral arrangement, he plucked out a flower, kissed it, and then tucked it behind Rebecca's left ear. "May I present Rebecca Baxter."

The king kissed Rebecca first on one cheek, then on the other. "May this union be blessed with many heirs," he replied in their native language, following the custom.

Rebecca smiled blankly, but as the king's words were repeated and swept around the room, a cheer went up. "What's going on?" she asked curiously.

He smiled. "My father has officially pronounced that he accepts our betrothal. You are to be my wife and the next Princess of Edenbourg."

* * * * *

CROWN AND GLORY

**Where royalty and romance
go hand in hand...**

The series continues in Silhouette Romance
with these unforgettable novels:

HER ROYAL HUSBAND
by Cara Colter
on sale July 2002 (SR #1600)

THE PRINCESS HAS AMNESIA!
by Patricia Thayer
on sale August 2002 (SR #1606)

SEARCHING FOR HER PRINCE
by Karen Rose Smith
on sale September 2002 (SR #1612)

And look for more Crown and Glory stories in
SILHOUETTE DESIRE starting in October 2002!

Available at your favorite retail outlet.

Silhouette®
Where love comes alive™

You've shared love, tears and laughter.

Now share your love of reading—

give your daughter Silhouette Romance® novels.

eHARLEQUIN.com

community | membership

buy books | authors | online reads | magazine | learn to write

magazine

♥———————————————————— **quizzes**

Is he the one? What kind of lover are you? Visit the **Quizzes** area to find out!

♥———————————————— **recipes for romance**

Get scrumptious meal ideas with our **Recipes for Romance**.

♥———————————————— **romantic movies**

Peek at the **Romantic Movies** area to find Top 10 Flicks about First Love, ten Supersexy Movies, and more.

♥———————————————————— **royal romance**

Get the latest scoop on your favorite royals in **Royal Romance**.

♥———————————————————————— **games**

Check out the **Games** pages to find a ton of interactive romantic fun!

♥———————————————————— **romantic travel**

In need of a romantic rendezvous? Visit the **Romantic Travel** section for articles and guides.

♥———————————————————— **lovescopes**

Are you two compatible? Click your way to the **Lovescopes** area to find out now!

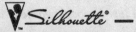

where love comes alive—online...

SINTMAG

SILHOUETTE *Romance*

COMING NEXT MONTH

#1600 HER ROYAL HUSBAND—Cara Colter
Crown and Glory
Prince Owen had once known love with beautiful American Jordan Ashbury. Back then, she'd fallen for the man, not the royal title he'd kept secret. But when she came to work in the palace kitchen five years later—her young daughter in tow—he found he wasn't the only one who'd kept a secret....

#1601 MARRIED IN THE MORNING—Susan Meier
Waking up in Gerrick Green's Vegas hotel room was embarrassing enough for Gina Martin, until she saw the wedding ring on her finger. She'd married the enemy—the man bent on taking over her father's company. But would love prove stronger than ambition?

#1602 MORE THAN MEETS THE EYE—Carla Cassidy
A Tale of the Sea
Investigator Kevin Cartwright was assigned to track down four siblings separated during childhood. Seeing Dr. Phoebe Jones on TV wasn't the break he'd been expecting, nor was falling for the shy, attractive scholar with a strange fear of the sea. But would the shocking mysteries of her past stand between them?

#1603 PREGNANT AND PROTECTED—Lilian Darcy
Being trapped beneath a collapsed building bonded newly pregnant Lauren Van Schulyer and a handsome stranger called Lock. Six months later, the mom-to-be met the man her father hired to protect her—Daniel "Lock" Lachlan! The single dad guarded Lauren's body, but he was the only one who could steal her heart....

#1604 LET'S PRETEND...—Gail Martin
Derek Randolph needed a pretend girlfriend—fast!—to be in the running for a promotion, so he enlisted the help of his sister's best friend, sophisticated Jess Cossette. But would the invented romance turn into the real thing for two former high school enemies?

#1605 THE BRAIN & THE BEAUTY—Betsy Eliot
Single mom Abby Melrose's young son was a genius, so who else could Abby turn to for help but a former child prodigy? Yet embittered Jeremy Waters only wanted to be left alone. Did the beauty dare to tame the sexy, reclusive beast—and open his heart to love?